"I was

Jonathan, in my own land, and my lovers were as numerous as the cells in a honeycomb. My people, the Sirens, had come to Crete in the Golden Age; come from their northern home to live in that southern land with the Wanderwooders, the Satyrs and the Dryads, the Leogryphs and the Telesphori. Wings to fly, legs to walk, webbed toes to swim: the ideal race, were we not?

"The ruined palaces of the Cretans, sprawling over the land and into the sea, gave us a home, a hive where a queen could rule her drones and workers and propagate the race. But we made of those half-sunken palaces a place of warmth and delight.

"I was only a child when the first Cyclopes came to the island. I had become a queen when they threatened you, my son of five years. . . ."

Thomas Burnett Swann

HOW ARE THE MIGHTY FALLEN

Illustrated by
GEORGE BARR

DAW BOOKS, INC.

DONALD A. WOLLHEIM, PUBLISHER

1301 Avenue of the Americas
New York, N. Y.   10019

FIRST PRINTING, MARCH 1974

1 2 3 4 5 6 7 8 9

Printed in U.S.A.

DEDICATION

To Adele Jergens,

The most beautiful,

Immortal in the marble of my mind

And it came to pass, when he had made an end of speaking unto Saul, that the soul of Jonathan was knit with the soul of David, and Jonathan loved him as his own soul.

• • •

Then Jonathan and David made a covenant, because he loved him as his own soul.

And Jonathan stripped himself of the robe that was upon him, and gave it to David, and his garments, even to his sword, and to his bow, and to his girdle.

—The King James Bible

Friendship is love without wings.

—Lord Byron, quoting an unknown source

Chapter
ONE

King Saul and his Desert Crawlers had met the Philistines at Michmash and routed the proudest army between Assyria and Egypt. The news had reached Ahinoam, Siren of Crete and Queen of Israel, as she traveled from the capital of Gibeah to the battle site. She approached the camp in a little ox-drawn cart with big wooden wheels which rumbled like a handmill grinding grain. (Horses were Hittite beasts, treacherous beasts, unfriendly to Israelites, untrainable, so it seemed to them. Camels belonged to the Midianites, as scrofulous as their masters. Oxen were slow but dependable.) Three attendants, an old woman, Naomi, who remembered Samson, and twin boys with little to remember but much to anticipate, accompanied her. All of them were much too tired to speak; it was hard even to walk, and from time to time Ahinoam had changed places with Naomi and allowed her to ride in the cart.

Ahinoam was prepared to find a celebration; she found a pervasive and unexplainable gloom. It was not that the men resembled ragged farmers instead of rugged warriors. She was used to the simple goatskin tunics they wore into battle, the cowhide shields and the shepherd staffs metamorphosed into javelins; accustomed also to the odor of the farm, the dirt, leather, and dung. But dishevelment was not the same as defeat. In the days when Saul had smitten the besieging Ammonites and freed the city of Jabesh-Gilead, bone-weary men had raised their voices in psalms to the glory of Yahweh and Saul. Today, in spite of a greater victory, despair was as tangible in the air as the brackish winds from the Dead Sea.

Rocks and rocky hillocks loomed at her oxcart like the formidable giants of Gath. In such terrain the Israelites had

9

won their victory, but her cart was built for roads, her oxen could not climb mountains, and Ahinoam, increasingly impatient, hailed the nearest soldier for details of the battle.

"We won a great triumph, my lady," he sighed, limping from an old wound.

"Why such a sigh, Caspir?" she asked, touching his shoulder with a slender, ringless hand. She knew every man in her husband's army, his wife, and the number of his children. "At Ramah they said the Philistines had fled to Askelon in total rout."

"Our king has forbidden us to eat meat or drink wine under pain of death. The Philistine herds are fat for the slaughter. Their supply wagons would feed our whole army for a month. But we must touch nothing, neither honeyed wine nor spitted lamb." Meat was a luxury in Israel. One of the rewards of victory was a celebration in which captured cattle—the Philistines had brought herds with the obvious intention of occupying the countryside—were slaughtered according to an ancient ritual and ravenously devoured on the battle site. "We fought valiantly for your husband, our king, but where is the man who doesn't hope for a share in the spoils of battle? We don't even dare to keep the little golden mice the Philistines dropped in their flight." The mice were amulets to protect their carriers from boils and the plague.

"Saul is in one of his dark moods?"

"Not dark, exactly. Darkening, I would say. Samuel has been sending him messages, and it was doubtless Samuel who suggested the edict: 'Let him who eats or drinks before nightfall be accursed by the Lord, and his curse shall be death.' Thus did the king exhort his troops. But the words have the ring of the Prophet, don't you think?"

"A day is a long time for hungry men," she said. "But the time will pass, and the feast will be better for being late." Though a queen as well as a Siren before she had married Saul, she was used to this poor little desert kingdom without fixed boundaries, and many times she had fled with her household before the advance of Philistines, Ammonites, or Moabites and lived for weeks on lizards and manna. She could not understand how gloom could have pervaded an entire army because of a senseless but minor edict, a short privation.

"Ah, my lady, that would be true if it were only a matter of fasting for a day. But Elim, the priest, slew *three good men* with his own hand. He caught them eating a bunch of grapes and smote them with the grape stains still on their lips. One was my cousin."

She shuddered and leaned for support against the cart. The brutalities of this country would never cease to appall her, of Israel no less than of its enemies, of Saul no less than of his less enlightened generals. (And men equated Sirens with cannibalism!)

"It was a harsh edict," she confessed. "I grieve for your cousin, Caspir. Saul is much changed these days." All of Israel knew of her shame and how she had been replaced in her husband's bed by the painted concubine, Rizpah. They also knew of the madness which grew in Saul like a black desert lichen and of the young shepherd, David, who sang to him in his rages or stupors and brought him a measure of peace.

Saul had not expected her to come to his camp at Michmash. He still recognized her as his queen, both in private and before his people, but for five years she had remained, a virtual recluse, in his fortified house at Gibeah. Her daughters, Michal and Merab, and her sons, Ish-Bosheth, Machishua, and Ahinidab, and whenever his father allowed him to leave the army, her oldest son, Jonathan, had kept her company, though the memory of giant wings, a sunken palace of amber and coral, fields of yellow gagea spread like a golden fleece, were a jagged shard in her heart. Now it was Rizpah, the concubine, whose tent, emblazoned with jackals after the custom of her land, was pitched beside that of Saul, and Rizpah's laughter which bubbled like the Jordan as it left the Sea of Chinnereth. But Ahinoam had come to Michmash not to visit Saul, she had come to visit Jonathan. He too had his bouts with a demon.

He was a great hero to his people, however, and, so Ahinoam learned from Caspir, he had never been more heroic than against the Philistines in the recent battle. Caspir had obviously memorized the tale:

"Under cover of darkness and accompanied only by his devoted armorbearer Nathan, Jonathan scaled the heights of Michmash held by the enemy. Remembering Gideon, he and Nathan broke pitchers, flourished torches, set fire to the

parched undergrowth, and sowed such confusion among the
enemy that they fell to fighting among themselves, and the
rest of us—outnumbered and armorless—climbed the hill
and easily put them to rout."

"Ah," she sighed. "Then he is safe. If only—"

If only Jonathan rejoiced in victory. How well she knew
that he preferred a hoe to a spear, a harp to a sword! After
every battle, a sorrow of cruel and penetrating clarity descended upon him, and he lamented the friends he had lost,
the enemies he had slain and for whom he seemed to grieve
almost as much as for his countrymen, and sighed, "All men
are equal in Sheol—shadows who mingle with shadows but
cannot speak."

She had come to solace him in his grief, and she earnestly
hoped to exorcise his demon.

The soldiers in the camp, as always, greeted her with a
fervor which never failed to pulse in her blood and quicken
the remnants of wings at her shoulder blades to a semblance
of flight. It was not merely that she was a queen and a
woman among a host whose king did not allow harlots and
wives to follow his army and pleasure his men after battle.
It was not merely that, in spite of her hundred years—a
secret withheld from everyone, including Saul and Jonathan
—she was incontestably the fairest woman in Israel. She did
not need or wish to flaunt her face or exploit her body. She
walked as artlessly as a maiden balancing a jar of water on
her head. She laughed like a young girl who has been betrothed to the boy she loves instead of the old man with
many herds. Israelite men—and most of them were natural
poets, in spite of their rough ways—liked to speak of Ahinoam in terms of bees and honey. Her backswept hair was
yellower than the bands of a bumblebee. She was redolent
of myrrh and pollen and, like the bees which help to pol-
linate the flowers, she was one of nature's handmaidens.
Finally, like every true queen, she possessed a sting. When
Saul replaced her with Rizpah in his heart and in his bed,
he looked as if he had met and barely survived a lion, and
his tent collapsed on a ruin of mats, pitchers, and weapons,
while Ahinoam, her robes in perfect array, departed with
the poise and circumstance of a visiting queen from Sheba.
Furthermore he found no sympathy among his people, and
Rizpah, the first time she visited the well at Gibeah without

attendants, was pelted with stones by the women of the town.

Why had Saul forsaken her? She could only conclude that the same qualities which had once fascinated him now made her an object of awe and terror. As a youth, he had listened with pride and wonder to her tales of Crete, the island of sunken palaces; desired her body, winged and alien, to the neglect of his people and the dismay of Samuel, the Prophet. Now, aging and graying, while she remained agelessly young, he preferred familiarity and comfort to passion. Furthermore, he often complained that she had no sense of guilt, and sin-ridden Saul, forever reminded of his transgressions by the ubiquitous Samuel, could not forgive her when she said, "What makes men happy is good. Your god has not *given* you laws, he has *shackled* you with them." She who at first had ensorceled Saul had ended by losing him to a frumpish and loving whore.

When Ahinoam arrived at Michmash, she had ridden for two days between hills whose only color was lent to them by the sun, a stain like the raw purple of an open wound; whose only vegetation was the lowly broomweed; whose only animals were gerbils and vipers. Water was powerless to quench her thirst, tincture of opium failed to ease her fatigue, though as always she looked like a queen. Blue starfish hung from her ears and dust of lapis lazuli twinkled in her sunbright hair. Her arms were discreetly covered to her wrists in accordance with local custom, but her silken sleeves were embroidered with blue sea shekels which Saul had mistaken for flattened loaves of bread! (Saul had never visited her lost island and her sunken palace, and only once had he seen the sea.) Her tiny feet, graced with sandals of ibex leather, looked as if they might flicker to magic pipes in the woods Beyond the World.

She refused, however, the usual adornments of wealthy Israelite women: the hennaed hair and fingernails, the ball perfumed with stacte and onychy between her breasts, the kohl for her eyes and the carmine for her lips. The faint coralline blush of her cheeks owed nothing to the cosmetic palette, and when she entered a camp she might have been an earthly incarnation of Ashtoreth. The wounded forgot their wounds; the hungry forgot their hunger; the prudish forgot that unescorted queens should at least wear veils when they visited armies.

"Honey Hair!" they called to her. "Honey Hair has come to heal us."

But where was Jonathan? Surely he had heard of her arrival in the camp. Quietly she moved among the wounded, whose cloaks must serve them as beds by night and garments by day. A physician, a harried little man named Anub, whose only badge of office was the herbal bag he wore at his side, hurried from blanket to blanket and consoled the dying with sincere but inadequate words.

"Opium will ease your pain."

"Your brother escaped injury."

"The wound will cleanse itself with the flow of blood."

In the old days Saul had permitted Ahinoam to join Anub and to heal his men with her simples and herbs and her Cretan incantations which sounded like the ringing of bells in a Philistine temple. But she was too successful even for a queen. The men began to ask: Is she truly from Caphtor, the island of green magic, the original homeland of the Philistines? Is she truly a sorceress? A goddess? A demon? Saul had hurried to banish sorcerers and witches from his land and forbidden Ahinoam to visit his men after battle.

He could hardly condemn her now, however, for seeking news of her son.

"The Queen Ahinoam honors us with her presence. Rebecca and Ruth would have paled beside her beauty." Thus the physician greeted her even while plying his trade. Anub had lost a hand in the siege of Jabesh-Gilead, but his remaining hand had smitten a hundred foes and healed a thousand Israelites, and he often boasted that Yahweh had spared him to the glory of Ahinoam, whom, like uncountable other soldiers, he quietly and hopelessly loved.

"I had hoped to be greeted by my son Jonathan," she said. Her heart beat as anxiously as a hare in a wicker cage. "Though it is very good to see my dear friend Anub, whose words gladden my heart." She might have crowned him, so eagerly did he clasp and kiss her hand.

"Your son Jonathan has won a singular victory."

"Why is he not in the camp to greet his mother?" He is wounded, she thought. Perhaps he is dead. Anub is afraid to tell me.

"Jonathan lingers among the rocks to see that no enemies remain to trouble us by night. And to tend the wounded who may have been overlooked when our soldiers returned to camp. His armorbearer, Nathan, is with him."

"Then Jonathan is in safe hands. Nathan would rather die than risk his master's life. Ask your men to raise a tent for me, Anub. After you have seen to the wounded." She turned to the boys who attended her, identical twins whose big heads gave them a humorous and faintly leonine aspect. "Will you share a corner of my tent?"

"If you please, my lady," one of the boys said—which boy she was never entirely sure—"we would rather sleep with the soldiers." It had not been easy for them, she knew, big boys and brothers, but not yet old enough for the army, to enter the camp in the company of a woman driving an oxcart.

She turned to Anub. "They will be safe?"

"Quite. This isn't a Canaanite camp, you know."

She dismissed the boys with one of those totally artless smiles which turned men's heads from other women, including their wives, and turned them to sins for which their jealous Yahweh might conceivably strike them with thunderbolts. Too young to respond as men, however, they withdrew with the deference which they might have shown to their mother. She resisted the urge to hug them against her breast and whisper such intimate words as a mother might speak to her sons.

Returning to Anub, Ahinoam said: "The women of Rizpah will fetch water for me."

"My lady, there are no streams at Michmash."

"Ah, this bleak and forlorn land! At least at Gibeah there are canals and vineyards. At least along the banks of the Jordan there are tamarisks and oleanders."

"But Jonathan found us water all the same," he continued, grinning and waving the stump of his arm. He spoke the name as worshipfully as one might have said "Michael, the Archangel." "Remembering Moses, no doubt, he smote a rock with his staff and out gushed water!" It was not a miracle. The porous limestone rocks of the area often concealed water. But to thirsty men in awe of Jonathan, the feat must have seemed miraculous. "We shall heat it in copper cauldrons that my lady may have a bath."

"And Naomi and I will lay a feast for my son."

"Rizpah's women will wait upon you."

"I will look to him myself. I have brought delicacies for him—leeks and onions, figs and manna cakes—and I would give him a quiet place to feast and to rest."

"Ah, my lady, he will feast indeed. None of us has eaten since sunrise. But the ban will be lifted with lamplighting time."

"First, I will see my husband. Has he retired to his tent?"

"With his new armorbearer, David. The boy is playing one of those old melodies from our wilderness wanderings."

If not Rizpah, then, it was David who comforted her husband, the young shepherd who could coax a lyre into music as sweet as the fabled glass chimes of Ophir. Even now she could hear the plangent melody issuing from Saul's tent. No matter. The music eased his spirit and she was pleased for him. Jealousy fell from her like an outworn cloak. Momentarily she remembered the old lost magic (so many magics, so long ago; but Saul was the last—except for Jonathan, who could never be lost to her).

"Send a man to announce my arrival, will you Anub?"

Saul received her with embarrassment but also with undeniable pleasure. She saw herself reflected in his eyes as that golden, lyre-tongued Lilith who had shared the Garden of Eden with Adam and Eve, and she smiled an inward, ironic smile because it was Eve, the wife and mother, she wished to be to him and not Lilith, the temptress. How old and worn he looked! Valor had gone from him with his armor; kingliness had departed with his crown, which lay on the floor like a child's discarded toy. She could have eased his spirit with songs of the sea, even as David sang about shepherds and pastures. Her hands could magic the wrinkles from his brow. But he had discarded her from his bed and his confidence, and she had entered the tent only to wait for Jonathan.

Rizpah, the concubine, sat beside him on a lionskin rug where loaves of bread, wineskins, bunches of grapes awaited the lifting of the ban. A clothes chest, carved from the cedars of Lebanon, sat against the wall beside a couch with feet like the hooves of a deer. There were no chairs. There was, in fact, little to indicate that the tent housed a king instead of a roving Bedouin chieftain. Even Saul's robe was unembellished, and its sleeves were faded and frayed. In the days of their love, she had sat at her loom for endless happy hours to weave him robes of Tyrian purple; to spin him cloaks as gossamer as the filaments of a silkworm's cocoon. Once . . . once . . . But what was regret except the foolish indulgence of one without hope? And Ahinoam hoped for Jonathan: good things . . . many things . . . neither thrones nor powers but freedom from melancholy and a love which was stronger than death.

The king rose unsteadily to greet her. He was not intoxicated, he was exhausted. David moved to support him, a boy with the face of an angel and the body of that particular angel who had wrestled Jacob. He stared at Ahinoam with a fixedness which would have been rudeness had it not been so utterly reverent. Ahinoam had met him recently in Gibeah and heard him sing and play. She admired both his voice and his psalms and she thought him the comeliest lad after Jonathan in all of Israel.

The two were opposites in other ways: David, small and sinewy, a lion cub not quite grown; Jonathan, tall and slender as a papyrus stalk. She thought of one in terms of an animal, the other a plant. One was created to fight, to wound, to defend; the other to fructify the mothering earth. When the cub had grown into a lion, he would be ruthless toward his enemies, of that she had no doubt. Would he always sheathe his claws among his friends? He had obviously charmed Saul; her daughter Michal had talked about him incessantly for a week. He and Jonathan had yet to meet, but if Jonathan loved him, then he was meant to be loved. For Jonathan, who was greatly forgiving, was also greatly perceptive of faults in those he met and in himself, the one person he had not learned to forgive.

Rizpah rose, smiled, and bowed. She was a dark-skinned Ammonite, her eyelids blackened with kohl, her arms ajingle with crude golden bracelets in the shape of serpents, too many of them, and too noisily jingling, her hair a flamboyant red from the dye of the henna plant. Neither beautiful nor, it seemed, intelligent, she possessed an ability which Ahinoam lacked: that of pleasing the king without appearing either subservient or assertive. Her entrance into a tent was a materialization instead of an intrusion. She was no more intrusive, in fact, than a three-legged stool, and far more comfortable. Ahinoam liked her for loving Saul.

Saul embraced Ahinoam with sadly feeble arms. She felt him wince when she touched a recent wound. (*Had I anointed him with myrrh and balsam, the wound would have started to heal.*) His pointed black beard, sprinkled with gray, was sharp but not unpleasant against her cheek. With a bow to his king and a smile to Ahinoam, David left the tent. His going seemed to quench a lamp. Still, she respected his sensitivity, so rare in one so young—seventeen, was it?—in leaving her to speak with her husband and soon, no doubt, her son. If only Rizpah had followed him! But the dark Ammonite returned to the mat of lionskin, her hair a garish tumult about her shoulders, and gazed at Saul with lovelorn eyes.

Ahinoam ignored the platitudes which Israelite women, queens no less than commoners, were expected to shower like manna upon their men.

"Where is my son?" she asked.

"Well and safe. As you know he is always the last to leave the field of battle. He lingers to study the countryside and the enemies' mistakes."

"And to find and tend the wounded, who are sometimes forgotten by the victors," she reminded him.

If David's going had seemed to quench a lamp, Jonathan's coming lit a candelabrum. Though doubtless wearier than any other man in camp, he laughed like a little boy at the sight of his mother and ran into her arms.

Jonathan was a princely paradox. He fought like an ibex, swift and agile, and compensated in skill for what he lacked in strength, for he was slim and supple rather than heavily built like his brothers and father. But he fought for Israel and to please his father, not for the pleasure of battle, and he was happiest in Gibeah, where he planted trees and read scrolls and played the lyre and enjoyed his brothers and sisters almost as if they were his own children, and worshipped his mother.

He was not attired for a royal court, even a court in a tent. There was sweat on his cheeks, dust on his garments, a scent of leather about him, and yet Ahinoam enfolded a wonder more rare to her than the gold and ivories of Ophir and held him in a long embrace. He was twenty and the idol of every virgin and most of the wives in Israel, but it was

often said of him that he fled an amorous virgin faster than
he pursued a Philistine.

He turned to greet the king and, forgetting the usual cour-
tesies, forgetting even to acknowledge Rizpah, started to talk
with tremendous animation.

"Father, I met your armorbearer, David, outside the tent.
We only spoke a few words but he will make a great warrior,
I think. He's still a boy, but he could have held his own at
Michmash. And before the battle, I heard him singing. The
men say he softened Yahweh's heart with his psalms and
brought us victory." Then, apparently realizing that praises
of David were not likely to concern a worried mother or a
weary father, he said to Ahinoam:

"You have ridden in the sun, Mama. Your face is burned.
You must put some balsam on it tonight. Still, the ruddiness
becomes you."

"And your hair is so dusty that I could mistake you for a
Hittite," she teased. "When you left Gibeah it was yellow as
a gosling." Ashtoreth be praised, she thought. For once he
has evaded his demon.

"I didn't pause to bathe when I heard you were in the
camp," he continued. He was notorious for his baths. The
men jested that he could not grow a beard because of the
frequency with which he washed his face. Yet no one except
his mother had ever seen him without his clothes, not even in
the streams where the men stripped and swam and sang
after a long march. It was said by some that he bore a terrible disfigurement across his back; by others that the mark
was strange and beautiful, a link to his mother and her
people on Crete or, in the language of Israel, Caphtor.

"And you were hungry and knew a feast awaited you."
She smiled. "A good dinner is stiff competition even for a
mother."

"I could eat a fatted calf, but it would taste better if I
shared it with my mother." There were few secrets, few
evasions between them, except when he fled into the tabernacle of his spirit, where even his mother could never follow
him. (It had been thus for almost half of his life. Once she
had found him in tears. "Why do you weep, my son?"
"Because I am like the sea." "How do you mean?" "It tries
to embrace the land, but the land hurls it back in broken

waves." He had fled from the room and left Ahinoam to
interpret his answer.)

"The sun is down," said Saul. "It is time to break our fast."

Rizpah stirred from her amorous languor. Silently she
moved between the guests and, with the help of flintstones,
lit the wicks which floated in terra-cotta cruses of olive oil.
The Philistines preferred candles, and those who had visited
Askelon or Gaza spoke of palaces and temples where great
candelabra hung from the ceilings like constellations and lit
the painted images of Ashtoreth until her eyes seemed to
glow like those of a cheetah. But Saul disdained luxury. He
still knew the seasons better than the manners and appurte-
nances of a royal court.

The flap of the tent rustled like the wings of an angry
raven. The lamps flickered with a sudden guest of breeze and
the aged priest Elim paused in the opening. For sheer per-
versity, he surpassed the petulant and senile Samuel. He
loved to predict a plague or prophesy a drought.

"There will be no feast," he announced in tones intended
to be funereal but, alas, as high and piping as a flute. "Someone has broken the king's commandment. Someone has drunk
or eaten before sunset."

Elim refused to move; obviously he hoped to arouse con-
sternation. Unfortunately he was a fat little man, bald and
big-eyed, who looked more like a Canaanite fertility god
than a priest of Yahweh.

Saul glared at him with his kingliest glare. "And may I
ask how you came to learn so dire a matter? Surely not from
Samuel. He is bedridden with the ague in the Sanctuary at
Nob." Saul was known to dislike the prophet Samuel, who
had anointed him king over Israel only to demean and
heckle him throughout his reign, resenting, no doubt, that
his own sons, who were liars and lechers, did not deserve the
throne. When to make war, when to make peace, when to
fast, when to avoid women: Samuel's list of prohibitions was
longer than that in the holy book of Leviticus.

"Why, from the oracle, how else?" Elim said. The oracle
at Michmash was an ancient terebinth tree whose branches
were hung with silver bells which, before the coming of
Yahweh, had been shaped like fishtailed gods or goddesses
with swelling breasts. Now they were merely bells; nevertheless, they managed to speak to the satisfaction of the priests.

"We shall go to this tree and hear for ourselves," Saul announced. He was not at ease with his god and he could not risk offending a priest, even a priest like Elim.

They followed Saul from the tent, Ahinoam leaning on Jonathan less for support than affection, since the mere sight of him, neither wounded nor melancholy, had rested her from her ride. He is pleased to see me, she thought, he is pleased at Israel's victory. But the joy which radiates from his body —I feel it like the warmth from a brazier—why, one would think that an angel had talked to him!

The oracular tree reminded Ahinoam of Samuel—old, brittle, skeletal, and lonely in its decay. It had died in a drought, when the Philistines stole the Ark of the Tabernacle from Shiloh, but bells still hung on its ancient branches, metal fruit on moldering limbs. Silent at first, they began to speak with the rise of the evening breeze. Even Ahinoam could hear the unwonted harshness in their tone. Usually they sang like crickets, but now they croaked like frogs.

Saul looked to Elim. "What do they say?" Deeply religious, he had not lost faith in Yahweh; rather, he feared that Yahweh had lost faith in him.

"Let the king discover and punish the transgressor."

Saul sighed and the years seemed to rest on his shoulders like a mantle of snow. Was this the ardent man she had loved at the well in Endor, he who had left his fields to raise the siege of Jabesh-Gilead and unite a divided country? It sometimes seemed to her that except for leading an army, which, with the help of Jonathan and an able cousin named Abner, he did with a skill amounting to genius, he hardly possessed the energy to sigh. It was her one satisfaction that he could no longer be an impassioned lover to Rizpah.

"Whoever has broken my commandment must die," Saul said, like a priest reciting a ritual. "Is it a servant among the baggage train?"

Again, the croak of the bells, a medley of fat, warty toads.

"A warrior?"

A listening silence fell upon the camp, and not only around the tree. Ahinoam saw that the warriors camped among the neighboring trees were watching the priest as raptly as the king and his retinue. They were starved in the midst of plenty. Their fires blazed readily to receive the calf or the lamb.

Their wineskins bulged with the juice of the grape and the pomegranate.

"One of my warriors?"

The tree resounded like the trumpet blast of an attacking army.

"But I have three thousand men! How shall I know the transgressor?"

"Let the king look to himself and his own family." Elim could not conceal his glee. He was known to resent Jonathan, Abner, Michal—all of those close to the king except Rizpah, with whom he liked to converse about the price of grain or a sickness among the herds.

A soldier and in the king's family . . . Only Jonathan of Saul's four sons had fought in the battle of Michmash. The other three sons, mere boys and much too young to fight, had remained in Gibeah.

"Jonathan, my son—" It was more a protestation than an accusation. Then, to Elim with growing wrath: "Do you dare to accuse my own firstborn?"

Saul's rages, which often preceded his madness, were the terror of Israel. He was known to hurl spears or demolish a tent or a room. Elim's confidence forsook him. He shrank like a threatened spider.

"The tree, not I, accuses."

"Perhaps I am guilty," said Jonathan. "I was not in the camp when my father delivered his edict. I have eaten no meat and drunk no liquid except water. But in the forest beside the desert—"

"What has my son eaten besides meat?"

"In the forest I came on a nest of bees. I ate of the honeycomb."

Everyone knew that Jonathan was loved by the bees. Often they led him to their hives and spun joyously when he partook of their wealth. It was whispered that Ahinoam had brought him, as a small child, from the island of Crete, where the bees built nests in the eaves of the ruined palaces, and the old demigods, the men with the legs of sheep, the women who lived in trees, danced by the light of the harvest moon and coupled to the piping of flutes and the clashing of cymbals. (It was whispered that he was not Saul's son.)

Saul's voice went dead, like a discarded lyre. "It was enough. Jonathan must die."

The words were hushed but irrevocable; at first they stunned instead of infuriated Ahinoam. Kings did not sentence their sons to death for eating a honeycomb.

"Then I must die."

"Die?" she cried. "What nonsense is this you speak, my son?"

"The sentence is Yahweh's," said Elim.

Anger flared in Ahinoam like a signal torch; against both of her men, the father too quick to condemn, the son too quick to accept.

She addressed Saul so clearly and contemptuously that most of the camp overheard her.

"Then you must also kill your queen. She has no wish to remain the wife of a king who would sacrifice his own son."

Even doting Rizpah protested the sentence. A foreigner like Ahinoam, she could not conceive the strength of an Israelite's oath to his god. "Surely my lord would not slay his firstborn and his finest warrior!"

"Abraham would have slain Isaac if the Lord had not stayed his hand." Saul's face was white and expressionless. It seemed to be hewn from the hard and savage hills which overlooked the Dead Sea like skulls. Even as she despised him, Ahinoam felt his pain and pitied him for his perplexity. He was a man with too many loves: his farm, his country, Yahweh, Rizpah, Jonathan, Michal . . . When they warred with each other, they weakened his will and allowed the demon of madness to enter his mouth and lurk in his brain, an invisible parasite.

"The Lord has demanded a sacrifice," a voice said so softly that its very softness compelled like wrath or indignation. "Let me die in Jonathan's place. I am only his armorbearer. In the heat of summer, when our swords are turned again into plowshares, I till the fields beside my brothers or tread the grapes. I have seven brothers. I will be no loss to Israel. Only to my mother and perhaps—perhaps—to Jonathan, who has treated me always like a brother. Jonathan whom I l–love." The boy stumbled over his words. He was not used to speaking to his king.

More than a king had heard him. The host of Israel, the men around the campfires, the guards patrolling the camp, shouted their indignation:

"Accept Nathan, spare Jonathan!

"It is Yahweh's will, or why did he walk with Jonathan on the slopes of Michmash?"

Saul looked doubtfully to Elim. "Is such a thing possible?"

"The Lord has been known to accept a scapegoat."

Jonathan's face was fixed with resolution. "It is I who have offended Yahweh. It is I who must suffer the punishment. Not my friend, who has loved me well and saved me from Philistine arrows and the bite of vipers."

"Enough of this, Elim. Ask the oracle if Yahweh will accept a substitute," demanded Saul.

The wind sang sulkily through the branches, the bells cooed like a flock of turtledoves, as if the tree remembered a greener time, a youth when she wore a mantle of fine-spun leaves instead of metal bells and received the rain like the sweet embrace of love.

"So be it," said Elim, grimacing disappointment. "Let Nathan die in place of Jonathan."

"It shall be done," said Saul. Large tears welled in his eyes; tears of gratitude.

Everyone looked to Nathan. A plump-cheeked boy with a slow, drawling voice, he was neither bright nor brave. But he was Jonathan's friend, and Jonathan hugged him with a desperate tenderness.

It was Saul who separated the youths. "It is time, my son," he said to Nathan.

Jonathan thrust himself between Nathan and Saul. "You are not to have him," he said to his father in a low but deadly voice. "He is my friend."

"Would you question the ways of Yahweh?"

"Yes, my father, I question his ways. Or rather, the manner in which you interpret them. I would worship a pitying Brother or Mother instead of a heartless Father who hurls thunderbolts to vent his displeasure and kills young boys for the mistakes of their masters."

"You're speaking like a Canaanite," said Saul with dignity but without reproof. Then, to his men, "Proceed with the sacrifice."

Six men struggled to keep Jonathan from his friend.

No men were needed to lead Nathan to the bloodstained stone beneath the tree or tell him where to lay his head or comfort him when Elim raised his knife. The boy spoke a single word:

"Jonathan."

Ahinoam looked into her son's face to seek the predictable pain for the loss of a friend. She was not prepared for the intensity of what she saw: anguish for the loss of a beloved.

Far away, at the far edge of the camp, a lyre trembled across the demon-haunted labyrinths of the night, and a single voice, yearningly sweet, a boy's voice, rose in a psalm of hope:

"Yea, though I walk through the valley of the shadow
    of death,
I will fear no evil:
For thou art with me;
Thy rod and thy staff they comfort me.

•   •   •

The Lord is my shepherd:
I shall not want.
He maketh me to lie down in green pastures:
He leadeth me beside the still waters. . . ."

Chapter
TWO

Before the battle of Michmash, David had visited the Israelite camp to bring food to his brothers, Ozem, Nethanel, and Elihu, who had fought with Saul for more than three years. At seventeen, he was forbidden by his oversolicitous father Jesse, familiarly known as the Ass of Bethlehem, to remain with his older brothers and fight the Philistines, though he had fought both the wolves and the lions which had harassed his flock.

"Linger in the camp only long enough to exchange tidings with your brothers," Jesse had said, sweetly adamant. "Elihu had a toothache when he left home and your mother is much concerned. Then return to your flocks. The battle promises ill for Israel."

In spite of the difficult walk, David did not protest; he
happened to like asses. Furthermore, he would glimpse Saul's
army and foresee the impending battle with a vision akin to
genius. The rocky terrain would help the Israelites; warriors
in sheepskin tunics could clamber among the rocks like desert
mice; warriors riding in chariots or walking in heavy armor
would long for the flat terrain beside the Great Green Sea.
Finally, heroic Jonathan was the captain of a thousand men.
David had never met him; once he had glimpsed him, the
swiftest runner in Israel, from a great distance and thought:
If Yahweh were such as Jonathan, I would become his priest.

David donned his one good tunic, blue Egyptian linen
embroidered with scarabs, and, at the insistence of his mother,
ran a tortoiseshell comb through his red, unruly hair. He was
not in the least aware of his appearance—the poppy-red hair
which he and no one else in his family had inherited from
Ruth, the woman of Moab; the small muscular body which
made him the envy of every wrestler in Bethlehem; the eyes
as blue as the waters of Lake Chinnereth. He was, in a
popular phrase, "as handsome as Sin," the Canaanite god of
the moon, and as indifferent to his looks as he was fastidious
in caring for his sheep, his sling, and his shepherd's crook.

When David arrived in camp with the cheeses and the
almond cakes patiently prepared by his mother, he hoped for
an enthusiastic welcome from his brothers, whom he loved,
and perhaps—who could say?—a chance to enter the battle
in spite of admonitions from a well-intentioned ass. After all,
he had brought the sling with which he had killed a lion
(small to be sure, but a killer of many sheep).

But the brothers were less than cordial. "Must we play
nursemaid to the runt even in camp?" hirsute Elihu had
sighed. David, who hoped that he would grow as tall as
Elihu, decided that he would grow like a trim cedar instead
of a shaggy tamarisk tree.

"Go about your business as usual, whatever that is," he
had answered, adding loftily, "I'm writing a new psalm."

"Write one about killing Goliath," Ozem said dourly. "He's
down with a fever demon. You'll know he's risen when the
earth starts to shake."

"I've heard he's twelve feet tall—"

"Nine."

"With legs like pillars in the temple Samson toppled."

"More like roof beams."

"And one big eye in the middle of his forehead."

"True enough."

"How is your tooth, Elihu?"

"Hurts like Sheol."

Then, with neither thanks nor leavetaking, Elihu, Ozem, and Nethanel departed to play knucklebones with their friends.

David did not intend to waste his visit to the camp by sitting on a pile of cloaks. Concluding that no one would care to steal such disreputable and odorous garments, he wandered among the men, carrying his lyre, his rarest possession, and explored the camp: the black sheepskin tents of Saul, Jonathan, Rizpah, and Abner; the roofless encampments of the foot soldiers. In Israel, every able-bodied man was a soldier during the Philistine invasions, but the rest of the time he was a farmer, a shepherd, or an artisan. There were few Israelite merchants; commerce was left to the sea-roving Phoenicians or the desert-striding, camel-riding Bedouins, who numbered among them the Midianites and other tribes.

"Get you home, son," said a man with a white streak meandering through his black hair like a rivulet through a desert. He had the keen eyes of a shepherd and the air of a man who is his own best company. He looked as if he would like to be tending sheep on the slopes of Mt. Hebron. "The battle promises to go against us, and they threaten to split our forces in the hills of Ephraim and the Judah Valley. Three thousand chariots, our scouts report! And nobody knows how many foot soldiers. You know how the Philistines fight." (Indeed, he knew how the Philistines fought; he had memorized every detail of every battle since the days of Joshua and Jericho.)

"But you have Jonathan," he said. Saul was a tolerable king, but he was aging and gray and given to moods which approached madness. Abner, the king's cousin, was a great general, but he was nearly as old as Saul, that is to say fifty. It was going to be Jonathan's battle. Three thousand chariots? Thus had Jonathan chosen a rocky terrain where the axles would crack on the rocks and the knives affixed to the wheels would blunt themselves on bindweed or thorny broom.

"Ah, what can a boy do against a giant like Goliath?"

"But Jonathan is not a boy!" (At *twenty*? Why, he was a

mature young man and the captain of a thousand men! Old
men liked to speak of anyone younger than themselves as
"boys.") "And I hear Goliath isn't with the Philistines," said
David. "And his brothers"—for Goliath belonged to the
family known as the Giants of Gath—"won't fight without
him."

"That's true. Even giants are subject to the demons of
fever, and when one of them is sick, the others panic and
refuse to leave their tents. But the Philistine necromancers
will doubtless exorcise the demons and he will be right out
there with the chariots. If not in this battle, then the next."
(There was always a next battle. It seemed to David that
Israel was engaged not in many little wars as the scribes
recorded on their scrolls of parchment, but in a large and
continuous war which moved from place to place and changed
its name but not its nature. It was much the same if they
were fighting the Philistines or the Edomites or the Moabites.
They fought to unite the Twelve Tribes of Israel, to secure
the caravan routes which passed through their territory, and
to gain access to the sea. Now if he were king...)

"It will take more than Jonathan, Yahweh help the boy, to
save us."

David withdrew as courteously as possible from this un-
congenial conversation. He did not like to hear his hero
regarded as less than heroic. He found a smooth black stone
for a seat—perhaps it had once been an altar, though the
Egyptians used such stones to make iron—and began to compose a psalm about Jonathan meeting a lion. He drew upon
his own experience, but he made Jonathan's beast a great
ravening brute with yellow teeth and slavering jaws; a worthy
foe for a great hero; and ended by becoming so enthralled
with his tale, which was both martial and bloodthirsty, that
he failed to notice the small crowd which had gathered around
him. When he finished his psalm—still unpolished, of course
—there was uninhibited applause from a dozen listeners.
Israelites loved music. They entered a battle to the blast of a
ram's horn; they had toppled the walls of Jericho with
trumpet blasts; they danced ecstatic dances to flutes when the
spirit of Yahweh descended upon them; and those who forgot
their own religion often participated in the fertility rites of the
Canaanites—the people who had ruled the country before the
explosive arrival of the Israelites—and danced until the fever

in their blood drove them to lie with strange women or, a particular abomination in Yahweh's eyes, with beardless youths as pretty as girls.

The next man who approached David was entirely gray, but he did not seem any particular age, even to a youth of seventeen. He seemed somehow beyond age, disease, death. He stood as straight as a shepherd's staff and his eyes were clear and blue and penetrating and his tunic was spotless and neatly spun of Egyptian flax. At first David mistook him for Saul, whom he had never seen close at hand (he never saw anybody important in Bethlehem).

Instinctively he fell to his knees. The man smiled; it was a kindly smile. There was a sadness about him, as if he had loved the wrong woman; David imagined him being scorned by a haughty Egyptian princess and sorrowing for her until he died. It did not occur to him that the man might simply be a farmer-turned-soldier like Saul who hated to kill.

"Stand up, boy. I'm not Saul, I'm Abner, the king's cousin. But I've come from Saul, who would like to hear you play. He caught some snatches of your song—something about a lion, was it?—and he wished for more."

"But I'm only a shepherd," David cried. "How can I play for a king?"

"You are a shepherd, it may be, but you are also a musician with a rare gift. The king is—how shall I say?—troubled. You might ease his spirit."

David was distinctly disappointed with Saul's tent. Somehow he had expected to find that the black sheepskin walls concealed the riches of an Egyptian palace, with naked temptresses languishing on marble couches, and a soft fountain spraying the air with myrrh, and trophies of battle, a human head on a stake, perhaps, beside the door. But it was, after all, only a warrior's tent and one which was furnished with a sparseness amounting to asceticism. A tired old man, clad in a gray robe without adornments, reclined on a wooden couch with no cushions, and a woman, painted but not provocative, bovine in fact, lounged at his feet. Saul's wife, of course, was neither in the camp nor in the tent. Since Rizpah had replaced her in Saul's affections, she had remained in the town of Gibeah, the capital, revered by her people even while she was rejected by her husband.

At David's entrance, Saul lifted his head and said, both

lucidly and kindly, "You're the young musician I heard. Will you play for me?" Then his head, with its sharp pointed beard, sank onto his chest and cobwebs seemed to pass over his eyes. He looked like a man exhausted with fever.

David looked at Abner. "What shall I play, my lord?"

"You may dispense with the 'lord,'" Abner said. "Play something about Yahweh and his forgiveness. The king has great fear of his god."

"Play something about Yahweh," Rizpah echoed, with the look of a ruminating cow. "Saul feels he has disappointed his god. He has not been harsh enough toward the enemies of Israel."

David and the entire country knew that when Saul was bidden by Samuel to smite the Amalekites and spare neither man nor woman nor child, he spared King Agag and it remained for Samuel to execute the Lord's command.

Such a stupid woman, thought David. How could Saul choose her above Ahinoam? Once only had he seen the queen and thought her carven from gold, so still and perfect she seemed, and yet with the heart of a woman, for he had seen her weep. (A boy with his herds, he had seen a tall, beautiful lady walking in the hills near Bethlehem. He had taken her for a goddess and feared to show his face. It was after Saul had sent her from his bed.)

David played a psalm which he had learned in his childhood. He played well because he pitied the king:

> "Like as a father pitieth his children,
> So the Lord pitieth them that fear him.
> For he knoweth our frame;
> He remembereth that we are dust.
> As for man, his days are as grass;
> As a flower of the field, so he flourisheth.
> For the wind passeth over it, and it is gone;
> And the place thereof shall know it no more...."

At first there was no response from anyone in the tent. He looked around him with sudden panic; he felt as if a lion, unseen but sensed, were poised to spring upon his flocks. How had a lowly shepherd from Bethlehem presumed to play for the king of Israel? It was then that Rizpah began to weep and Saul raised his head. The king stared fixedly at David through eyes no longer clouded; indeed, they had become judging, calculating, concluding. He was a basically simple man, David decided, forced by the duties of kingship into complexities which would baffle the wisest of pharaohs. He must lead an army; he must rule a court; he must pacify the Lord and try to placate Samuel. Now, thought David, humble beneath the cool appraising stare, he must even judge a shepherd's performance with a lyre.

"You must play for me again," said the king.

"I have to return to my father tomorrow," said David. "He sent me here to bring some cakes and cheeses to my brothers."

"Your father, you say? Jesse of Bethlehem, is he not? I know him well. A good and loyal subject who has sent me three of his sons. Can he not spare a fourth to please his king?"

David reconsidered the invitation. "I have four other brothers at home, and a sister to help my mother." The chance to hurl a spear as well as play the lyre was irresistible. "It may be—"

"Consider it settled," said the king. He smiled, and the perfect white teeth looked strangely young in the scarred and aging face. The pointed beard usually gave him a fearsome aspect, but now he appeared indulgent, Yahweh after he had fashioned the earth and taken his ease on the Seventh Day.

"He is too young to fight," Abner said firmly.

"I have need of an armorbearer. Let him first learn his duties in the camp. Only then shall he go into battle. Meanwhile, he can play his lyre for me in the evenings."

Rizpah smiled winningly—her mouth was large and her teeth were blackened from chewing betel nuts—and she offered David a tarnished silver bracelet which she stripped from her wrist. There were no coins in Israel; business transactions were made on the basis of produce, copper ingots called shekels, or bracelets of metal and stones. In short, she was paying him for a performance.

David shook his head. "I did not play for hire."

Abner smiled and clapped him on the back. "Rizpah intended a gift, not a payment. But young boys, especially armorbearers to kings, need tunics and sandals more than bracelets." He ushered him from the tent. "Later we will find you a corner to sleep in. And fresh garments. Go now and get your things. You have pleased the king greatly. But always remember. His moods are as changeable as the desert—and as dangerous."

"I'm not afraid. Will I get to meet Jonathan?"

"Jonathan is often with his father. He will no doubt help to instruct you in your duties."

"I would like that," David said.

"Would you?" said Abner, musing. "Jonathan has need of friends."

"But he can have any friend he chooses. He's the hero of Israel!"

"It is very lonely to be a hero, especially at the age of twenty. He needs someone who will talk *to* him and not *up* to him."

Thus David became Saul's armorbearer, but before he had learned to fight, the battle of Michmash was fought and won by Jonathan's stratagem and Abner's strength and only a lack of supply wagons and chariots prevented the Israelites from pursuing their foe to the sea. After the battle, David cleaned the iron-tipped spears of the king and his son. The metal was new to Israel, but the two spears had been captured from the Philistines.

"Enough of that," said the king. "A child can clean a spear. Only David sings like Gabriel."

He sang the psalm which he had written for Jonathan, and Saul seemed immensely pleased to hear his son applauded as the hero of such an adventure. Even as he sang, David attempted to further understand his king: You would rather be flailing wheat on your boyhood farm than ruling a court. It is neither pride nor vanity which drives you, but dedication. You feel that you have inherited the mantle of Joshua and Gideon and must recapture the Ark of the Tabernacle and restore the glory of Israel. Thus your pride in Jonathan and thus, because you are human, your preference for a harlot over a queen, since the one time when you can be a simple man instead of Yahweh's emissary is in the arms of Rizpah.

David's brothers made fun of him when, as they said, he "caught a man in a tent" and evaluated him to the last precise detail of appearance and character. But David's tents were carefully raised and staked.

"Jonathan will be honored by your song," said the king.

"He is a great warrior, is he not?"

"The best in my army next to Abner."

"I envy him then."

"Don't."

The word was abrupt and unanswerable. The king, seeing David's surprise, tried to explain his terse command.

"Great warriors may become great victims. The enemy seek them out in the press of battle. Jonathan is very young. If he should die, all of Israel would mourn him like a bereaved maiden."

But David sensed another meaning behind the words. Jonathan unenviable? (*I will meet him and judge for myself if he is truly great and truly fortunate.*) Leaving the tent when Ahinoam arrived to await her son, he encountered a young man with a dusty tunic and the face of a god.

Even through the dust, David discerned the torrent of golden hair, brighter than sunlight on a wave; the faintly slanted eyes, blue as the waters around the Misty Isles (so landlocked David imagined); the perfect lips, faintly pink like the lip of the conch shells used by the Philistines as horns to begin a charge. (*Strange to think of him in terms of the sea. I have never been to the coast.*)

He discerned too a surprising weakness in the famous young warrior. It was neither moral nor ethical; it was not a shifty eye or averted gaze. Rather, there was a fragility about him; he was like a purple murex with its delicate spines and its exquisite dyes. He is too beautiful, David decided. He has about him the transience of perfection. Being already perfect, he cannot be improved, he can only be broken.

"You are David," said Jonathan. His smile would have warmed Goliath. "A demon of fever kept me in my tent before the battle. But I have heard of you."

"How did you know me?"

"By your lyre, of course. But most of all by your face. Your red hair is the talk of the camp. It is like the hills of Judah at sunrise." Israelite men, unlike the Philistines, did not as a rule speak of masculine beauty; only of skill or courage or strength. "My father says you play like an angel. Won't you stay now and play for me too?"

"No—no," David faltered. "The queen, your mother, is waiting for you." Never had he wanted so much to stay. Never had he wanted so much to flee. He is like Ahinoam, he thought, with one difference. She, though rejected, remains a queen in the citadel of her pride. He is without defenses in his gentleness. Thus, it is Jonathan who is the greater threat to me.

Jonathan laid a lightly restraining hand on David's shoulder.

"Soon then?" The fingers were slender and supple. There were no calluses, yet the hand had held a sword which had smitten many Philistines and would, it was hoped, smite Goliath when the giant returned to the fray.

"Soon. Now you must go to your mother."

He fled from Jonathan's presence, but it was not easy to flee from his spirit. . . .

He met his brothers where he had been appointed to guard their cloaks. Elihu grumbled. "Our brother is a better watcher of sheep than sheepskins."

David was not in a mood for criticism. His brothers had neglected him when he arrived in the camp. Quite on his own he had become the king's armorbearer, met a queen, and befriended a prince. Now he would repay them. Just as he never forgot a kindness, he never ignored a slight.

He said loftily, "The king has summoned me. I am going to become his armorbearer."

The brothers stared after him in amazement as he strode toward Saul's tent with the manly stride of a seasoned warrior. But the face of Saul, noble and fierce and yes, pitiable, loomed in his mind, and he felt the terrors of a bridegroom going to meet his betrothed's father for the first time.

When he reached Saul's tent, the occupants had departed to the sacred tree. Standing in the shadows, David heard Elim's accusation of Jonathan and Saul's judgment. If Nathan had not anticipated him, he would have offered himself as the scapegoat.

He heard Nathan's anguished cry when the knife pierced his heart, but he felt much more keenly the knife of reproach in Jonathan. Because he did not dare to visit the grieving prince at such a time, he composed a psalm for him, and Jonathan was the speaker. The words seemed to come of themselves, and the shepherding lord was youthful in his thoughts and not a bearded Yahweh, a brother instead of a father:

"The Lord is my shepherd, I shall not want.
He maketh me to lie down in green pastures. . . .
Yea though I walk through the Valley of the shadow
    of Death,
I shall fear no evil
For thou art with me. . . ."

"David."

"Has my song pleased you, Jonathan?"

"It has greatly eased my spirit. Does Yahweh sorrow for Nathan, do you think? With all the great heroes like Moses and Joshua, has he time to worry about a little armorbearer?"

"Yahweh or another," said David, before he realized that he was speaking heresy. "It is always the smallest lamb who needs the most protection."

"Perhaps the Lady of the Wild Things," said Jonathan. He, too, then believed in other gods than Yahweh.

"Ashtoreth?"

"Ashtoreth is only one of her names. To my mother and me she is simply the Goddess or the Lady. Your song may have reached her ear, if not Yahweh's."

"But I wrote the song for *you*."

"Did you, David? You promised me a song. I didn't suspect how soon."

"But you thought I would keep my promise?"

"I knew."

"Can we talk together?" asked David, emboldened by Jonathan's grief and the need to solace him. "I have only my cloak to offer you for a seat. Perhaps there is a corner in your father's tent?"

"We can go to *my* tent." Jonathan's tent; the tent of mysteries. Few had entered that sacrosanct place, that haunt of creatures unimaginable: a bird of lapis lazuli that sang real words; a living bear whose fur was white like the snows on the summit of Mt. Hebron; and secret things. Forbidden things. Forbidding things?

THREE

"I don't have many visitors." Jonathan smiled. "I hope you'll like my tent."

"I want to see your bird—" David blinked and saw more than a bird. His brothers had led him to expect gigantic Baals and Ashtoreths with breasts as large as coconuts; censers burning with aphrodisiac myrrhs; naked maidens with carmine on their nipples. It was not that young, beardless Jonathan suggested such lecheries. But the brothers argued, "He is much too gentle for any man. No one can be so good. No one can be so chaste. Not even Samuel before his sons betrayed him and he became a sour old man. Not even Saul before he left his farm to become king and began his fits of madness. Jonathan hides his vices in his tent. . . ." Needless to say, they and almost every other man in the camp admired his secrecy and envied him his supposed vices: men who were bored and homesick between battles and missed the chatter of their wives and sweethearts; grizzled fighting men bewitched by a youth they loved and followed but could not understand.

Indeed, the tent was miraculous, but its miracles were those of a child. Wind chimes shaped like little girls in bell-shaped skirts tinkled and danced in the breeze from the open flap. Coquina-colored boxes in many shapes and colors, like the blocks of a Cyclops' child, twinkled on the floor. A box as high as your ankle for holding sandals. A box as high as your hip for a seat and pillowed with stuffed lions and deer. Jonathan, like a little boy who had found a treasure in the woods, and wished to show a friend, a rare butterfly or an orange mushroom, lifted the lid of a large circular box and proceeded to remove and open a smaller box, and so to the seventh and smallest, which held a big green bumblebee.

· He handed the bee to David. "Watch out. He stings," he said in an ominous voice.

David dropped the bee as if he had already been stung. Jonathan smiled and returned the bee to its nest of boxes. (*But why does he never laugh?*)

"He's not real. He's carved from a tourmaline. My mother says the dolphin folk carved him, before their arms became flippers."

Miracle succeeded miracle. A wooden fennec, crudely but lovingly modeled from clay, stood on his head, and his feet held an oil lamp in the shape of a coconut. A terra-cotta hyena—a highly unpopular animal in Israel—sat on his haunches and begged a bunch of grapes from a wooden shepherd boy who looked disconcertingly like David. Live animals, too, frolicked among the boxes with the freedom of the woods: a gerbil, a hare, and yes, a small white bear who collided with his master and raised his snout for a pat of forgiveness. Jonathan stroked his fur.

"Go to David now. He's my friend."

The bear advanced upon David with a look which could only be called inscrutable.

"Is he going to bite me?" David asked. He was used to the large brown bears which sometimes threatened his flocks.

"Mylas likes you, and he doesn't like many people. He's very old, you see, and cantankerous, and wants to be left on his goatskin rug except when it's time to eat. Or when I come from a battle and he licks my wounds and helps them to heal. He liked Nathan too, but you and Nathan are almost the only ones. He bites every woman except my mother. Once he tore off Michal's robes and bit her on the backside."

In spite of the reassurances, David did not expose his rear. "Where did you get him?" There were no white bears in Israel except Mylas. Had he come, like a phoenix, from the Woods Beyond the World?

"He came to me from the sea," Jonathan said without explanation. "And as for my bird," he added, unlocking an ivory cage and lifting its occupant of lapis lazuli, which he handed to David as if it were mere crude clay, "he's for you."

"For me?" David cried. "He's a gift for a king!"

"Of course," laughed Jonathan. (*But he never laughs with his eyes.*) "Why else would I give him to you? Keep him in the cage except when you want him to sing. No one will try to steal him. He's bewitched against thieves. Hold him in your right hand. Caress his head—so—with your left hand."

The bird began to sing, quietly at first, and with notes instead of words.

"It's the music of Ophir," said Jonathan. "Once a great queen of that land visited Philistia and loved a seren of Gath. At last she had to return to her own country. 'My heart will break when you leave, like a piece of coral in a stormy sea,' he said. But she answered him with a gift: 'Wherever you go, my bird of lapis lazuli will speak for me, and you will be companioned.' And he took the bird and was never without her."

"How did you get him, Jonathan?" He liked to speak the name: Jonathan—"gift of the Lord" (or the Lady?).

"I met the seren in battle, oh, long before Michmash. I was just a boy at the time. The seren was wounded but he could still have killed me, since I was also wounded and very weak. He was too kind, though. The Philistines aren't a cruel race. We fight them because they keep us from the sea. The seren and I helped each other into his tent. 'You remind me of my son,' he said, 'and I am going to let you live. But I have a wound which will be the death of me.' He opened a casket of yellowing ivory—the old kind, very rare, from Ophir. 'Here, take this bird and think of the man who loved you as a son, though he saw you only once. At the proper time you will understand.' "

The quiet notes became words, and the words were an incantation.

> "Bird from the Wanderwoods,
> Transfixed in flight
> By lapis lazuli,
> Blue heron
> Climbing like my thought
> To bluer height,
> And open-mouthed in cry
> No bird
> Has heard,
> When you alight
> In that blue land,
> Will I,
> Will I?"

Roughly David returned the bird to its cage. "It's too much for you to give me," he protested, though he could not explain his unease. The song had charmed him with its strange, bell-like endings. There were no rhymes in the songs of Israel.

"What the heart gives is never too much."

"You never gave the bird to Nathan, did you?"

"He would have liked a flute or a shepherd's crook. I saved the bird for David, who perhaps can understand its song."

"But we only met today. I'm not even sure if I understand *you*."

"Once in a dream, I saw a boy with red hair and big, strong fingers which could coax magic out of a lyre—or choke a lion. We walked together in a field of chrysanthemums, and he understood my heart."

"Do you have second sight?" asked David, puzzling over the dream.

"Sometimes," smiled Jonathan. "My mother has it more often."

"They say," David ventured, "they say that your mother is a sorceress or a goddess and she came from Caphtor, the Island of Green Magic."

"I don't know," said Jonathan. "I truly don't know what I am or where my mother came from. Does it matter?"

"It makes me afraid of her."

"And me?"

"A little at first. Not now." It was Jonathan's power to make the wonderful familiar or, just as effortlessly, the familiar wonderful. He was not like those witches and sorcerers who frightened or threatened you with their magic; he was not even like his mother, who seemed to have no enemies, but also no intimacies except with Jonathan.

"I was afraid of you too, David. Afraid for you to read my soul and perhaps turn away from me. You see, there is so little time. At night I seem to hear the thunder of chariots and feel the terrible grinding of their wheels."

"But you are the son of the anointed king!"

"Am I, David? And does that mean that I will one day rule in Israel?"

"Yes, and in Philistia as well, perhaps."

"Some men are meant to rule kingdoms. Others—"

"To what?"

"To love."

"And you've loved, haven't you, Jonathan?"

"Not as I would choose."

"Why, half the women of Israel—wives included—would lie with you."

Jonathan's eyes did not waver. "I do not want to lie with the women of Israel or any other land."

"Not even the virgins with breasts like pomegranates?"

"Least of all the virgins."

The thought unsettled David: that any young man would avoid a beautiful virgin except out of fear of her father! How would Jonathan get an heir to the throne and perpetuate Saul's line?

"You're afraid of being unclean in the eyes of Yahweh? But he only requires that a man keep himself from women before battle."

"I do fear him," Jonathan admitted, "but not for the reason you think."

"And you've never lain with a girl?"

"Never."

"Or loved one?"

"I love my mother and my sisters. I loved an old woman who used to make my tunics for me. And there was a little girl in Gibeah who brought me a bunch of daisies before every battle. Both of them died of the White Sickness."

"You know what I mean."

"Never," sighed Jonathan. "My mother says that the highest love is a circle, not a crescent. The crescent moon—friendship or love for family—is pure and silvery. But the full moon is orange and abundant and includes all the lesser loves in its circumference." He paused. "I've never known a full moon myself." He placed a hand on David's shoulder, like a little bird—perhaps a sparrow—which the least movement would frighten into flight. "Seek your full moon, David. Leave the crescents to me." He spoke like an old man, with resignation if not bitterness. Did all warriors talk so sadly before or after a battle? Perhaps the death of Nathan accounted for his gloom.

He took Jonathan's hand and pressed it against his cheek. He was a boy who liked to touch the things he loved, to feel their textures and their emanations, whether they were objects or people, a wooden slingshot or a friend's hand. The fact that the hand belonged to a prince did not disturb him in the least.

"Your friend died quickly—and he died for you. It was a good death for him, I think. He chose to take your place because he loved you."

"I envy him," said Jonathan.

David stared at Jonathan with disbelief: the slender body, swift and deadly in battle and yet, in his tent, as vulnerable as the bird in the ivory cage. He looked at the sad and perfect smile, like the smile of a sculptured young god who appeared to have known all loves or, being a god and therefore beyond men, no loves.

It was wrong, it was terribly wrong for such a man to be sad! Impulsively he enfolded Jonathan in his arms, as if the prince were a lost sheep he had rescued from the wolves, and felt the frantic beating of his heart. He felt too the soft projections from his shoulder blades, almost like rudimentary wings. Was Jonathan a changeling?

Somehow he jarred the bird of lapis lazuli into his song, and the song, after all, was a spell.

> "When you alight
> In that blue land,
> Will I,
> Will I?"

Indeed, the prince he held in his arms had suddenly become a sheep which bleated and licked his face! Before he could drop the beast, he held a girl with yellow hair and the tail of a fish and laughter which sang like the surf in the wind. If he dropped her, she had no legs to break her fall.

It was a smiling Jonathan who wriggled out of his arms and stood in front of him on two distinctly human legs.

"You—you are a necromancer," David blurted. "But your father has banished such men from the land."

"I don't turn into sheep before my father."

"Or fish-tailed girls who look like female Dagons?"

"Nereids, you mean. I don't really turn into anything. I just make you think I do."

"You have bewitched me. My brain is befuddled. I can hardly stand."

"Then I will help you to find Abner. He will give you a place to sleep."

"But we've just begun to talk," David cried. He did not want to leave such magic, however unsettling to him, a shepherd whose friends talked of nothing more magical than the number of sheep in a herd. He did not want to leave a prince and a magician for the cold company of his brothers.

"I am tired," said Jonathan distantly. Laughter had left him, and left him, it seemed, indifferent. "Perhaps you can find your way alone. Your dizziness will soon pass. It was wrong of me to tease you."

"Couldn't I—couldn't I stay here with you?"

"It is not allowed. You are my father's armorbearer, not mine."

"Good night, Jonathan." He *would* speak the precious name. He *would* rouse the prince from his unaccountable indifference and recall the happy child.

"Good night, David. Don't forget your bird."

"I don't want him," said David stubbornly. "I only wanted him because he was a gift from you, and now you're sending me away."

"David, my brother. . . ."

As unexpectedly as a desert mirage, Michal appeared in the tent. David had met her with Saul and Rizpah. Being the daughter of a man who was both a king and a general, she was used to the ways of men; she was a bold and blithe-hearted girl, ready with a jest, quick with a knife, but neither brazen nor coarse. She lacked the gold of Jonathan and Ahinoam; she did not make you think of a honeycomb or a lark or a cornucopia. But she was the young green buds on the terebinth tree in spring. She was both the loveliest and the liveliest girl David had ever met. Once—yesterday in fact —he would have liked to kiss her and he had dreamed of taking her in a plowed field.

Now he resented her intrusion.

"David," she urged him. "Stay and break bread with my brother and me."

Around her neck she wore an image of Ashtoreth. Not the swollen-bellied mother of the Canaanites, but the slender lady of the Philistines, the lady of love who placed not a single prohibition on lovers, either of age or sex, except that they love with their bodies as well as their hearts, their hearts as well as their bodies. According to an old Philistine philosopher, "The body is the temple of the heart. How shall we reach the sacred image unless we enter the gates?"

Forgetting that she was a princess of Israel, forgetting even to nod, he brushed past her and fled toward the tent of Saul. In the shadow of another tent, he saw the figure of Ahinoam, hushed and amber in the light of many fires. She scarcely moved her lips and yet he knew that she was smiling to him.

He knew also with surprise but without shame that it was Ashtoreth, not Yahweh, who had been with Jonathan and him in the tent.

Chapter

FOUR

She stood in the opening to Jonathan's tent and softly called his name.

"Come in, Mother," he answered in a faint voice. He rose from his couch, only to slump on a mat of reeds and, like a little Bedouin boy, fling his arms around his knees. He refused to look at her, but stared at the far wall of the tent, black goatskin above a cedar clothes chest, as if he could find an answer in its shaggy night.

Ahinoam knelt beside him and placed an arm on his back; smelled the scent of him, the fragrance of grass and leather; yearned to hold him and rout the demon of melancholy which, after Nathan's death (and David's visit?), had returned to torture him.

"Half the women of Israel are in love with you," she said. "The other half want to be your sister or your mother."

"And I must wed and produce a male child to inherit the throne. Father has told me as much a hundred times."

"You must do what is in your heart. If you do not choose to wed—"

"I chose to die in place of Nathan, my friend, but little good it did me."

"Let me tell you a story."

"Stories are for children." He looked like a frightened child.

"What about this one? You are not Saul's son."

"Not Saul's son . . . ?"

She could read his thoughts: Not the son of a marauding desert chieftain who believes that to rule means to conquer cities or to take a concubine and father stalwart sons. . . .

"Whose then?"

"You are twenty but you haven't a beard."

"I don't want a beard. It would be dangerous in battle. An enemy could seize it and cut my throat."

"Other Israelite boys grow beards long before they are twenty."

"It will come in time." He shrugged. "What has that to do with my father?"

"Look at my back." She bared her shoulders and stood in the light of a large lamp, a cruse of oil with seven wicks like the tongues of salamanders.

"Wings," he gasped. "Like mine."

"Did you ever wonder how you got them?"

He struggled to speak his thoughts. "When I was a small child, you taught me never to show them. A deformity, I thought. Or worse, the work of a demon. I supposed the others would kill me if they knew. Samuel would hack me to pieces as he did King Agag and then blame Yahweh."

"They are natural characteristics of your race. In the Golden Age, our wings were built for flight. Now they are petty things. But all things dwindle in these paltry times."

He looked incredulous. To an Israelite, a creature with wings was either a demon or an angel. The demon was wicked; the angel, terrifying and full of Yahweh's wrath.

"Have you never wanted to fly?"

"Haven't all men?"

"No. Some men want to sail ships to the Misty Isles or the Dusky Sea. Others, like Saul, want to trample enemies and raze cities. When they catch one enemy, they find another."

"Mother," he pleaded. "Tell me who I am." His eyes were green and questioning. The forest was in them, the fresh new green of spring-awakened grass; shy, tentative, not yet assured of winter's departure. The ocean was in them, halcyon-still above a reef of coral.

I was a queen, Jonathan, in my own land, and my lovers were as numerous as the cells in a honeycomb. My people, the Sirens, had come to Crete—the island you call Caphtor— in the Golden Age; come from their northern home to live in that southern land with the Wanderwooders, the Satyrs and the Dryads, the Leogryphs and the Telesphori. Wings to fly, legs to walk, webbed toes to swim: the ideal race, were we not? But we had angered the Goddess and she had driven us from our palaces of sculptured propylus; stunted our wings and shut us from the sky; exiled us to the alien south. Still, I was a queen. Honey Hair I was called.

Before we came to the island, human men had lived in harmony with the Wanderwooders. Kindly men, the original Cretans and their allies, the Philistines, who worshipped the Goddess with libations of milk and decked her forest shrines with seashells and anemones. But earthquakes toppled their palaces and drove them to flee to the mainland in their goose-prowed ships.

After our exile, we had swum from the north to Crete; without ships; without tools; weary, homeless, hapless. We did not build new palaces. The ruined palaces of the Cretans, sprawling over the land and into the sea, gave us a home, a hive, where a queen could rule her drones and workers and propagate the race. Stone columns bristled with barnacles. The great facades, leaping with bulls and worshippers, had cracked in the sun. Field mice had burrowed where Cretan youths had danced the Dance of the Cranes. No longer could you hear the jangle of the sistrum like the shake of a coin pouch, the beat of drums, the rustle of belled skirts on flag-stones, the chatter of blue monkeys in the enclosed gardens of lotus and papyrus. But we made of those half-sunken palaces a place of warmth and delight. We glazed the walls with the rich red clay of the island and painted frescoes of our northern home, the forests of fir and pine, the fleet-toed deer; we swam in the sunken rooms and festooned the floors with seashells and bits of amber and climbed on the ledges to dry our golden hair; we tended herds of sea cows to give us milk and loved them almost as much as the dolphins with which we played.

I was only a child when the first Cyclopes came to the island. I had become a queen when they threatened you, my son of five years.

"Mama," you cried, springing into my arms from the giant tortoiseshell from which I had made your bed. "What is that terrible roar? It sounds like a Minotaur."

"A Cyclops, Bumblebee." That was my name for you before I came to Israel.

"A giant?"

"Yes, the sons of Poseidon, the sea king. They stand as tall as a mast and peer through a single eye at a world which seems to them created only to be destroyed."

"Can he hurt us?"

"Not as long as we have our palaces and spears, and our bears to warn and guard us."

"Let's show them we're not afraid. Let's walk in the forest and look for mushrooms! We'll tiptoe so the Cyclopes can't hear us."

It seemed to me then that the Goddess had forgiven my people: she had given me you. Doubly armed, I with a spear, you with a little knife, both of them dipped in the venom of the Jumper, that deadliest of spiders, we stepped into the light. I felt like a morning glory as it greets the sun. The workers, as always, toiled at their various jobs, returning with nectar from a field of saffron crocuses; manufacturing wax with the help of propylus secreted from their mouths; storing honey against the winter sleep. The drones, arm in arm, meandered through the avenues where Cretan gallants had walked in the smile of the Goddess. At the mating time, when buds were greening the winter-forlorn trees, they would follow me in the nuptial flight—or swim, I should say, since the punishment of the Goddess denied us the sky—and I would choose as my mate the drone whom I wished to crown. We would meet and embrace and my consort, stricken by love, would fall like a broken boat to the bottom of the sea, even while his soul ascended to the Celestial Vineyard. Meanwhile, the drones must seek each other for love. My workers lived only for work. Neither did they beget children nor receive lovers, but the drones were passionate beings, and who was I to deny them the love of their friends? The Goddess never decreed that men should lie only with women. All of the races which worship her—the Wanderwooders, the Cretans, the Philistines, the Canaanites, the Phoenicians—accept the love between two men as one more affirmation of the divine plan, the tide which rises and falls to the moon's compulsion, the inevitability of the seasons, the certainty that those who love will meet, after death, in the Celestial Vineyard. A man's love for a man is neither more nor less than a man's love for a woman, it is only different.

"Honey Hair!" A young drone with a white tunic caught by a belt of tourmalines had called my name. He was small and trim like an ivory dancer from the workshop of the Sea Kings. His name, Myiskos, meant "Little Mouse." He released the arm of his friend and bowed to me.

"Yes, Myiskos?"

"Please don't leave the hive without an escort."

"My spear will keep us from harm, my son and me."

"Beautiful things get broken."

"Dear Little Mouse," I said. "Perhaps I will choose you for my next king."

He smiled wistfully. "If only you could choose Hylas at the same time. Even the Celestial Vineyard would seem lonely without him."

I looked at the young drone who was waiting for Little Mouse. Like most of his friends, he was smooth and beardless, with a saffron glow to his skin. But his tunic revealed a sturdy frame; he was quick with a spear, strong to wrestle, swift to swim. It is folly to think that men who love men are mincing and high-voiced like the eunuchs of Egypt. More often they are brothers in battle, comrades under the deaf, indifferent stars.

"I could not spare the both of you."

They resumed their walk and paused to examine a flower which had sprung between the cobblestones.

"A mustard flower," said Hylas. "I am glad that our sandals did not crush her."

In perilous times they could speak of flowers. Yet, under attack from the Cyclopes, they were valorous warriors; the two of them fought as one.

It was good to walk in the forest, among the yearning oaks which remembered the reign of Father Saturn, that wise old king who, it was said, had nested swallows in his mosslike beard. The latticed branches formed a wizardry of light and shade. Woodpeckers drummed against Dryad oaks.

"Mama, let's visit Alecto. I can hear the breakers. We're near her home."

Alecto was also a Siren, but she was a solitary queen, like the bees which never build hives. She spent her time in the sea disporting with dolphins or lying on beaches where the crackle of shells would warm her of an approaching Cyclops.

An oaken wilderness yielded to a carob grove, cultivated by the Cretans, now forsaken along with a summer house of blue-rimmed windows and a rusting bronze plow. Beyond the grove, the land fell away to purple rocks, where the tide, withdrawing, had bared a multitude of treasures and trifles— murexes with fragile spines; starfish with broken legs; flotsam from the foreign galleys which sometimes plied the coast. I held your hand and we clambered over the rocks until the waves broke at our feet in diamonds of foam.

"Out there lies Philistia," I said. "Sometimes her sailors still return to this island, once their home. And beyond them, so I am told, are the Israelites, a race of warrior-farmers led by a young king named Saul."

"I want to go there," you said, staring across the green, disheveled waters. The look in your eyes was old and wise and full of journeys; it was the way of our race, sometimes, to remember what we had never seen, and to foretell what we were yet to see.

Then we spied Alecto, the Siren called Silvergilt because of her hair, which looked like foam in the sun. She had heard our approach, recognized us as friends, and continued to sun her tresses on a rock. She opened her arms and you dropped my hand and pressed your face against her opulent breast. You liked her scent of foam and ambergris. I tried to hide my concern. It was the solitary queens like Alecto who, in our northern homeland, had eaten some little sailor boys and brought upon us the wrath of the Goddess, to say nothing of a bad reputation with mariners.

She reached to her throat and removed from her necklace a tourmaline in the shape of a bee, which she presented to you as a gift.

"It came from the sea," she said. "A treasure from the dolphin folk. It will bring you luck one day."

She released you with some reluctance, rather as one foregoes a banquet, and turned to me.

"Honey Hair, I'm glad you've come. You see, I'm going away."

"Where are you going?" I cried, envious of her free and wandering life.

"To Philistia. Perhaps to Israel."

"You can't fly," I reminded her.

"I'll swim. It will take me at least a week. But I can rest on the sea like a gull."

"You were close to tears. You did not want to lose your friend. "Don't go away from us, Silvergilt!"

"Dear little Bumblebee, I have to go. A Cyclops killed my sister Electra only last week."

"The Cyclopes," I repeated, shuddering. "Yes, they are dreadful beasts. I fear for my palace at times—"

"Only if you scorn us."

The voice boomed and reverberated among the rocks.

"Goliath," Alecto screamed and, quick as a diving gull, she dove in the water and disappeared in a maelstrom of foam. Clutching you by the hand, I sprang after her; I beat my wings in frantic flurries and barely escaped Goliath's hairy fist as it slapped the sand behind us even as we reached the surf. He waded into the water up to his hips, but in spite of his parentage, no Cyclops can swim; heavy as elephants from Nubia, they sink at once to the bottom of the sea. Remember how Polyphemus stood on the shore and hurled boulders at Odysseus' ship He couldn't swim after him.

"Come back to me, Honey Hair," Goliath pleaded with a voice which tried to be intimate and succeeded in being sinister. His single red eye glowed like an open wound. "We have no females. The Dryads are much too small and most of the Sirens have fled the island. I would give my eye for a woman like you."

At a safe distance from the shore, I treaded water, you beside me, both of us more curious than frightened, and studied his features. His hair was matted with sores and dirt. He seemed all mouth and eye; mouth ferocious with crooked teeth, eye unblinking and cold as an undersea cave. He reminded me of a shark.

"Your hair is spun out of honey," he said. "Your breasts are ripe pomegranates." Cyclopes pretend to be poets, but they steal their metaphors from our Siren songs. The stench of him, dried blood and goat's hair, wafted over the waves. He ought to write scurrilous satires, I thought, instead of lyrics.

"Mama, let's go home," you pleaded. "He smells like a goat."

"If you trouble me again," I said, "I'll gouge your eye with my spear."

He wrenched a stone from the beach and hurled it into the sea to splatter foam in my face.

In the following days, day turning into month, spring ripening into summer, Silvergilt did not return to the rocks beside the sea. She has swum to Philistia, I thought. She has made her escape. But I must see to my hive.

Meanwhile, the time had come for the Dance of the Bears. The bears or Artori of Crete were our special friends in the forest, our allies against the Cyclopes and other beasts. Small, white, and delicate in appearance, disconcertingly fierce when aroused, they worshipped the Goddess in a ritual dance performed on the shortest night of summer, and we inevitably and joyfully joined them. The workers remained in the palace. To them, dancing was idleness and sin. But the drones, Myiskos and Hylas among them, were prompt to accept the invitation in spite of a threatened storm, and the bears greeted us as if I had promised them a glimpse of Honey House, the place where they go after death. We met in a meadow trodden by the hooves of Satyrs.

"I will play the flute," Myiskos cried.

"And I will beat the drum," said his friend.

To accompany flute and drum, the forest blended her many voices: wind in the branches of carob trees, stream carousing with rocks and fish, thump of woodpecker beaks on aged oaks. Even the plain little nightingales opened their throats in the songs which were their one loveliness.

The bears began to dance. Heads swayed from side to side. Left foot to the left. Right foot to the right. Return. Repeat. Advance. Retreat. White fur in the light of the moon. Molten fur in a sea which expanded, shrank, pulsing as if to the moon's commands. I watched you join the bears, agile among the dancers, and laughed as if baby Pan had joined the festival.

"I watched you join the bears, agile among the dancers."

Then it began to rain. It was one of those sudden rains which rapidly become a tempest. Lightning made of the sky a great parchment of bold hieroglyphics.

"Boreas out of the north," I cried. "No more dancing tonight." I tried to shelter you from the big cold drops.

The bears scrambled for shelter among the trees. Fearless of Cyclopes, they feared the lightning above all natural dangers because it singed their fur.

"Myiskos, Hylas," I called. "Back to the hive."

"*Honey Hair!*"

I knew the voice before I saw the face.

Goliath stood in our path. The noise of the storm had hidden his approach. The rain and trees hid most of his body, but I saw that his red eye had fixed me in its baleful glare.

Remembering wings, I whispered around him, you in my arms, and fled toward the hive, only to see a sight more terrible than a Gorgon's stare. The palace was under attack. The workers were making a gallant defense with their poison spears, but Cretan palaces have no walls, and the bears had scattered among the trees. I looked behind me for Myiskos and Hylas, who had waited to wrap their musical instruments in cloths against the storm.

Myiskos raised the stick with which he had beaten the drum. It was a pathetic weapon. Goliath snapped it between his fingers and clutched Myiskos around the waist. Hylas ran at him with no weapon but his flute, which he tried to use as a dagger; Goliath, whose skin was as tough as that of a Hydra, seized him with his free hand, thrust him above his head with Myiskos, and flung them against each other and then to the ground.

What must I do? What could I do? I could not get to the palace. I could not save my drones. I could only save my son. The sea, I remembered. The sea . . . Jonathan can swim like a fish. . . .

It was my last sight of the hive. I thought that the waves would shred our wings. I thought that weariness would turn us into lead and sink us among the crabs and the Hydras. But we did not fight the waves, you and I, we rolled with them; we used them to buoy us like two little boats. Thus we rode with the storm, long, long—how many turns of the hourglass?—scarcely using our arms and legs.

The storm subsided like a placated god. The Great Green

Sea enfolded us in his silver fleece: whitecaps, spray, the aftermath of Poseidon's wrath. Had he sent the storm to conceal the attack of his sons, the Cyclopes?

We could not see our island.

"It's that way," you gasped.

"I know," I said, but the current swept us inexorably from our hive, our home.

There were halcyon times when we rested between the waves. We lived on seaweed and, being Sirens, drank the water in spite of its salt. It was a dangerous journey, it was a desperate journey; but the current, at first inimicable, became our friend and carried us toward the mainland and the coast of Philistia. . . .

We climbed from the sea and fell, exhausted, onto a bed of broken shells.

"Mama," you asked. "Where are we?"

In the distance, a city coruscated with slender temples and laden wharves, goose-prowed ships and cockleshell fishing boats. Around us, white sand was punctuated with wizened bushes of sea-grapes and driftwood as black as timbers from a burned galley.

"Philistia, I think."

"Will the Philistines shelter us?"

"I'm afraid they would take us captive and put us in cages to show in their temples."

"You mean they would show us off? You, a *queen?* Silver-gilt said they were like the Cretans."

"It's true they came by way of Crete from their northern home. And they are kind. But all human peoples take slaves. Even we have our sea cows to give us milk."

"Why don't we swim home?" you asked.

"Because," I said, "I have hurt my arm."

I fell asleep and awoke to a sharp pain and a fierce hunger, and you, like a little harvest god, presenting me with a cluster of sea-grapes.

"You've slept all day," you said. "Eat now, Mama."

"Yes, you must both eat." The speaker was a young woman who had darkened her eyes with kohl, ruddied her cheeks with the powder of the insect called cochineal, and reddened her hair with the dye of the henna plant. Even her voluminous robe could not conceal her enticing figure. I mistook her for a Philistine courtesan until I saw the sea in her eyes and recognized a considerably altered Alecto.

"Silvergilt, you've hidden your wings and dyed your hair! I must call you Scarletgilt."

"It's just as well, Honey Hair. Wings mean death or slavery in this land. The Philistines will worship you but lock you in a temple. The Israelites will take you for a demon, since you are too beautiful and the wrong sex to be an angel, and probably stone you."

The sight of her metamorphosed from a free-living Siren into a human-appearing prostitute saddened me almost out of the gladness of seeing her.

"What shall we do?" I sighed. "Bumblebee and I." Even a queen, particularly when she has lost her palace and her kingdom, can ask advice.

"What I did. Hide the marks of our race. Become one with this land. Only three months ago I arrived on these shores. Look at my feet."

Her sandals of kidskin revealed toes without webs. "A simple operation with a knife removed them. As you know," she added with a disconcerting smile, "solitary queens like me have always been expert with cutlery."

"You live among the Philistines?"

"No. I've stayed here on the beach since my arrival. The first day I met a young warrior who had come to net murexes. 'The cost of purple dye is prohibitive, except to kings,' he said. 'Yet Philistine warriors like myself are expected to wear a purple tunic on feast days and a purple plume into battle. I shall make my own dye.' At first he mistook me for a daughter of the fish-god, Dagon, and offered, indeed threatened, to carry me to his priest in Gath. I persuaded him to change his mind. When military duties called him back to his garrison, he left me his tent and sent me robes and jewels by way of his friends, who invariably lingered for a night's refreshment. After him, there have been not only warriors but fishermen, merchants from Phoenicia, and even Israelite shepherds who owe fealty to Philistia."

"All in three weeks?"

"A night with me is worth a year with the best wife in the country."

"But don't your lovers die in the act of love?"

"Drones disembowel themselves and of course they die.

But human males are constituted for many acts and, I must add, they seem to improve with practice. Think of it, my dear. Every evening a nuptial flight, and with a *practiced* male, not a callow drone. When there are no young men— and I do insist upon youth, even though I am, as you know, upwards of a hundred—I work my arts of sorcery for the old. I conjure the dead from Sheol, a region of brackish streams and tongueless ghosts, the place where the Israelites go when they die. The spirits are glad to answer my summons and leave such a dreary region, if only for a look or a few words exchanged with a mate or a friend. Thus, with my two occupations, I can live near the sea and still pass for a native. I was walking along the seashore miles to the south when I heard you call."

"But I didn't call."

"Your spirit did. I knew you needed help. You and Bumblebee there."

"But my toes," I hurried to say, "and my wings—"

"I will give you toes like mine. As for your wings, you must simply keep them hidden. They are very small; Israelite robes are very loose and concealing. Even if you intend to become a courtesan like me, you will have no problem. As for myself, I give my lovers a potion of forgetfulness—sea nettles crushed with the inky juice of the squid. Thus they forget my wings but remember me. It's all in knowing the right dosage. Too much and they'll forget everything. You may do the same—after I clip between your toes."

"And Bumblebee?"

"Easier still. At his age, he won't even feel the pain of my knife. And you can teach him never to show his back."

"It means we can never go home. How can we cross the sea without webbed feet?"

"If you wait till your arm is healed, you can certainly never go home. And what is home anyway with the likes of Goliath skulking about the place?"

"Yes. The Cyclopes. They've probably captured my palace, killed my people, and eaten my sea cows."

"But Mama, what about the Celestial Vineyard?" you cried. "We've left the island of the Goddess. The god of Israel may send us to Sheol."

"I suspect the Great Mother will still look after us." It was a doubtful hope; we had angered her once in our northern home and she had sent us wandering to the south. Now, we had left her island for a country where deserts outnumbered forests. But Alecto possessed a genius for survival, and her advice, though unpalatable, was certainly practical.

"Whatever you say, Mama." You looked, however, with longing at the sea and fingered your stubby wings as if they, like the webs of your feet, must also face the knife.

Alecto smiled at you with sympathy. "I will give you my potion to make you forget the past."

"Must I forget?"

"Yes, my dear. The memory of Crete, the sea cows and the white bears, would only haunt you in this dismal land. Do you want to stay with me, you and your mother, here by the sea?"

"I think I had better take him inland," I said quickly. "I rather fancy the Israelites, from what I have heard. I like farmers—men who are close to the earth."

"I must find you some cloaks before I lose my business. A look at you and your nakedness, Honey Hair, and—well, I would earn silver while you earned gold."

I had quite forgotten that Bumblebee and I had shed our garments at the start of our swim from Crete.

"Down the beach a way, there's a camel caravan out of Midian. But first, your toes."

In Alecto's tent, I drank of sleep, you of forgetfulness. Awaking, we found the webs removed from our toes. You knew me to be your mother but did not know the past.

"My toes hurt, Mama," you said, "and I have a pain in my head. Where *have* we been?"

"You've had a fever," I said. "You walked in your sleep on the beach and stepped on some jagged shells. I ran after you without my sandals." You did not ask me about the remoter past. It was the power of Alecto's drink.

She returned at dusk. I thanked her for what she had done to earn the cloaks, the shekels, the provisions for our trip—dates, cheese, bread, waterskins, and a vial of her potion in case I should choose to follow her trade. The cloaks smelled of camel, but they were loose and comfortable against the heat, and our new sandals did not press cruelly between our toes.

We stayed with Alecto for a week. Then, jangling shekels in a money bag, we began our journey to find a home. We traveled by night and rested by day. In seven days we crossed the border into Israel and reached a small village—one of those forgettable and featureless villages of clay and straw-thatched huts clustered around a well—and we lingered in an inn which was little more than a house whose attic was rented to wayfarers. Dressed like the villagers—I in a white ankle-long robe trimmed with malachite-green, with a veil to hide my face; you in a goatskin tunic—we spoke little and seemingly escaped notice. The language of the place was a dialect of the same tongue which was spoken on Crete, in Philistia, and by the Israelites. Daily, at dusk, I visited the village well. On the fifth day a young man arrived on foot, accompanied by a small contingent of soldiers who looked as if they would rather be farmers. Israelites. I could tell from their pointed beards. In their ill-fitting tunics, they hardly seemed a match for the armored Philistines. But there was earth in their look. They were close to the soil. They were men who could predict the rain by the flight of quail or snow by the thickness of fur on a fox's back. I liked them, and more than liked their chief, who stared at me as if he were trying to guess the features beneath my veil. I lifted the veil to drink from the well and gave him a generous look.

"By Yahweh," he gasped. "It's Eve out of paradise!"

He walked toward me with purposeful steps. Boldly I met his gaze. A simple man but brave; a man to trust.

Of course it was Saul.

* * *

Her story ended, Ahinoam stared impatiently at her son and waited for him to speak. Have I eased his heart, she wondered, or tortured him with another guilt?

"Did you tell him who we were?" he asked finally. "Or did you give him the potion like Alecto?" Even as the lamp-light flickered across his high cheekbones, his faintly slanted eyes, an inner radiance equaled the reflected light of the lamp. It was the bright and wounding light of innocence.

"I told him. After I had won his heart."

"What did he say?"

"He was too besotted with me for reproaches. I knew that he was horrified—a woman with wings, a Siren!—but fascinated too. He asked me only this: that I should marry him but give you another draught of Alecto's drink. He wanted you to think him your father—he liked you at once, it seems.

We never spoke of the matter again, not even when I bore him, from time to time, the eggs which hatched to become your brothers and sisters. All of them were human in every way, neither wings, nor webs, nor troubling memories, nor eyes and ears in their brains. They know the legend, of course, that you and I are from Crete. But they know better than to ask questions."

"Who was my real father?"

"A drone named Meleagros. It was he who gave you the green of your eyes. I loved him more than Saul."

"But how did Saul explain us to his friends?"

"He said that I was a widow from Ophir and you were my son. The Midianites had stolen us from our house. But we had escaped in the desert and found our way to Endor and the well—and him. No one believed him, I think. But Saul was a king. Who were his men to deny his tale? Except in the whispers which have encompassed the land, and made us, you and me, an intriguing legend which even Samuel does not dare to attack."

"And you never knew if Myiskos and Hylas were dead?"

"No one has ever survived Goliath's blows."

"But they died together, didn't they? That is something, at least."

"Yes, and perhaps we will meet them in the Celestial Vineyard."

"Not Sheol?"

"Not that gray anonymity. Sheol is for the wingless."

The veins stood blue and prominent on his clenched fist. "You think I am like them, don't you?"

"I don't know. If you are, I am not ashamed. In the eyes of the Goddess, the only sin is unloving."

"I loved Nathan, the shepherd. But he was a brother to me, or so I thought."

"Who can say that any love between the young is entirely of the flesh or apart from the flesh?"

"The sins of Sodom—"

"Sodom was neither better nor worse than any other city in this desert land—Israelite or Canaanite. An earthquake destroyed it, not the hand of Yahweh."

"It may be true," he said. "But there won't be any more shepherds for me."

"Won't there, my dear?"

Chapter

FIVE

The recent victory at Michmash belonged to the scribes. The routed Philistines had returned to ravage the land, and Goliath was now their champion in the Vale of Elah.

Most of the night he had ranged the opposite bank of the stream which divided the two armies and, prodigiously drunk on Philistine beer, hurled obscenities and thick-tongued defiance. He did not know of Ahinoam's presence among the Israelites. If it were not for Jonathan's fever—Jonathan whom she had come to nurse—she would have fled on foot or by ass at sunrise and closeted herself in the fortified house at Gibeah. Fear of his lust was a dryness in her throat, like a breath of scorching sand from a sirocco. But he threatened more than her person; he threatened to lose her the trust of the Israelites. Rumors that she had been a queen in Caphtor, the sometime home of the Philistines, had failed to harm her, for her loyalty to Israel was beyond question. But the knowledge that she was a Siren would enrage and terrify a people who believed that women with wings, unlike men and angels, were descended from the cruel and seductive Lilith. She could imagine Samuel inveighing against her: "A witch, a temptress, abhorrent to Yahweh! Stone her before she ensorcels more than the king. . . ." If only they knew how she loathed the beast Goliath! How once, as a girl, she had met him in a forest on Crete and . . . (Ashtoreth, spare me from memories, she prayed. But Ashtoreth had other concerns) . . . oak trees grew tall around her, and sunlight dappled her tunic of ibex fur.

She had found him kneeling beside a stream and studying

his image in the clear water. He was so repulsive—indeed, he shuddered at his reflected self—that she wanted to touch and reassure him. His people were newcomers to the island. They had come on a huge raft with a sail—a dozen of them —and no one knew at the time their homeland or customs or gods.

"Are you afraid of me too?" he asked. "Everyone else is."

"Bears can be big but they don't frighten me."

"Come and show me your necklace. I never saw such lovely stones."

"Amber," she said. "Alecto, the Siren, gathered the bits on the floor of the sea. The tears of the Nereids."

His huge hands tentatively moved toward her—she did not run—to fondle the beads. How gentle, she thought. His hand is as big as a shield but his touch is butterfly-soft.

"Now you are my prisoner," he smiled, cupping her between his hands. "I will build a house for you in the woods and keep away the wolves and the Night Stalkers."

"And I will cook you tunny and sea-grapes," she laughed, for she was a child at the time and fond of games, "and keep your house as clean as a beaver's lodge!"

Finally she saw the evil behind his eyes. It was rather like looking into a sea cave and finding, deep in the shadows, a malevolent shark.

"But first I must get my robes and my comb and another pair of sandals. You don't want a slattern to keep your house!"

The odor of him was rank in her nostrils.

"Honey Hair." The fixed and frozen smile became a leer. "I've heard them call you that. Come with me now. You won't need robes with me." The shark had emerged from his cave.

She uttered a sweet piercing cry which echoed through the trees and over the beach and under the sea like the song of a nameless bird. He threw her to the ground and spread her arms and her cry became a scream. . . . It was the Artori who saved her. The forest suddenly bristled with living bushes, and bushes became bears, and the bears snapped at his heels until he fled among the trees.

"Honey Hair, one day I will crush your petals and drink your nectar!"

Would he recognize her and remember his boast?

She dozed briefly and then stirred into consciousness; the rough animal-hide walls materialized around her. The smell of goatskin permeated the air; the couch was hard and pillowless; there was sand in her hair from the journey which she had made without preparation and without attendants on the back of an ass. Almost instantly, however, she dismissed such minor hardships from her mind. . . .

"Jonathan is ill," the runner had said.

"I know my way to the camp," she had answered. "Stay here and rest in Gibeah until you recover your strength."

The Vale of Elah was not a desert like Michmash but a valley of palm trees and acacias and a stream of pure melted snow from the mountains. For more than a month the Israelites and the Philistines had faced each other across this stream, equally matched and readier to exchange insults than spears. It was the return of Goliath, cured of fever, which had destroyed the balance.

She had visited Jonathan immediately on her arrival and found him feverish and incoherent in the grasp of demons, while the kind but inept physician bled him with leeches. She had instantly recognized the nature of his attackers. They were Bedouin ghosts to whom leeches were no more objectionable than gnats. They were not killers, these Bedouin dead, but troublemakers, jealous because they must dwell forever invisibly among those places where, in life, they had roistered and robbed and worshipped no gods except the moon and the stars.

She kissed Jonathan's brow—how hot he felt!—and momentarily he recognized her.

"You should not be here, Mama. *He's* here and I must fight him."

For an instant she thought: He remembers Goliath from Crete. But no, he knew only what the men had told him about the foreign giant, engaged as a mercenary by the Philistines. Quickly she gave instructions for the preparation of a medicinal drink.

"Jonathan," she said, pressing his damp hand. "Repeat these words after me." His voice was hardly audible but hers was strong and clear; the star spirits would surely hear her and perhaps turn from the Bedouins.

"Chant the astral formulae;
'Deneb and Aldebaron,
Capricornus, Scorpio,
Wheel in orange, wheel in blue,
Whirl the stellar sorcery.'

Hail the crescent courtesan
Climbing halls of indigo
(Orange is her sickle shoe):
'Wrest the lunar sorcery
Onto them assaulting me.' "

Unexpectedly he relaxed and smiled and pressed her hand. She lifted his head and forced him to drink a bitter concoction of sour wine, gall, myrrh, and opium which was poisonous to the demons. Shadowy figures like great bats flapped above his couch and passed immaterially through the roof of the tent. Thus, she eradicated his pain and fever but left him too weak to accept Goliath's challenge.

Across the stream, Goliath boomed continual obscenities. "I will crush the tent of Saul beneath my fist. Hyenas will feast where I have walked. Gibeah will shudder at my approach. The queen of Israel will lose her gold."

And what would he think of her "gold" after fifteen years, the last time he had seen her on Crete; the years when a small boy grew into a young man, a devoted husband clove to a painted whore? It was not vanity that reassured her, nor the bronze mirrors from Ophir, but the mirrors in men's eyes. She had grown not old but ripe, as a green apple grows scarlet or amber or saffron. Her hair outshone the gold of the acacias, her body glowed beneath her encumbering robes as if she had bathed in pollen and drunk nectareous wines and become one with the various mosaic of the Goddess.

But what had beauty brought her except rejection and exile? If she had remained the favorite of Saul, she might have brought peace between Philistia and Israel. She might have convinced him that the Philistines were not the brutish and warlike people of popular fancy. The men were tall, beardless, and slender, the women fair of skin, with russet hair which they twisted above their heads in the shape of beehives or conch shells. Their villas beside the sea were little memories of their old Cretan palaces. They drank from cups as delicate as eggshell and painted with dolphins or starfish. They lifted food to their mouths with silver spoons instead of fingers. Ladies with lilac parasols walked to the goose-prowed ships to greet their returning husbands or watch the unloading of tin from the Misty Isles. True, their country was small and they must expand to survive, even as the Israelites, or go the way of the faded Hyksos, the fading Hittites. But Philistia with her ships and sailors and Israel with her robust farmers, united by treaty, could have founded colonies in foreign lands, or farmed their own lands with canals and aqueducts and tripled the produce.

She would have been stoned, however, if anyone had guessed that she admired the Philistines for their love of the sea and for the graces which go with such love, even as she admired the Israelites for their closeness to the earth and a ruggedness which approached grandeur.

But it was almost time for Jonathan to wake. I will carry him wine, she thought, in a minuscule amber cup like a bumblebee, and a loaf of bread, and a mouse's portion of cheese. I will nourish him into health but prolong his recovery, so that another champion may challenge Goliath. Hastily she robed herself in a gown embroidered with green leaves and golden figs—Saul thought it rather shocking, Saul liked his women in grays or browns—and she did not take the time to don a headdress or veil or even to comb her hair, which fell about her shoulders in the manner of a young bride, nor to perfume herself with frankincense or nard. She was much too concerned about Jonathan.

She stepped from twilight into the fresh spring morning. The Philistine tents were clearly visible across the stream. She gasped at the sheer number of them, like so many rainbow poppies in an unplowed field. She had to remind herself that they harbored death. The warriors were moving freely among their tents. Clean-shaven and armorless, they looked to her more like boys at play than warriors ready for battle. Unlike the Israelites, who learned to fight before they learned (if ever) to read and farmed when they did not fight, the Philistines fought by decree, not choice, until they were twenty-five, and then, unless they felt a special affinity for war and conquest, devoted their lives to voyages of exploration and trade or to the arts and the crafts which they had brought from Crete. They were slender Jonathans, not husky Davids, and it was hard to hate them when she heard the

jokes which they exchanged with the Israelites whom they
were soon to fight or drove their lean bronze chariots between their tents like boys preparing for a race.

For once, however, they had chosen the battle ground. For
once the Israelites could not escape into craggy passes and
lie in wait for an armor-burdened enemy to lumber after
them.

"We must not fight at Elah," Abner had pleaded with
Saul.

"The Lord, not the Philistines, has chosen the place,"
Samuel had answered. "He will raise up a champion among
you." Samuel, however, had carefully avoided the field, complaining of an ague. It was often said of him that his advice
had wings but his body preferred a nest.

Nevertheless, the Philistines had hesitated to cross the
stream and attack the Israelites, such was the reputation of
Saul and Jonathan and Abner, and the fact that the Israelites
now had the weapons and armor captured at Michmash.
Then, in a space of three days, Jonathan had caught a fever,
Saul had succumbed to his demon of madness, and Samuel's
prophecy had been ironically fulfilled: the Philistines, not
the Israelites, had raised a champion. Goliath had joined
their army.

Though her own camp was stirring around her and men
were beginning to stare, Ahinoam paused and remembered
the place, the Vale of Elah, and drank her surroundings as
one might drink red wine. Groves of light, feathery acacias,
half bush, half tree, flaunted their puffy balls of yellow
flowers and made her think of tiny suns in a green firmament.
Almond trees vied with acacias and, though their pink and
white blossoms had briefly bloomed and died, their burgeon-
ing green leaves made her wonder why the tree was called
"the hair of the old"; it should be "the hair of the Dryads."

Male francolins whirled in black and white above her head
and the females, sober in brown or gray, resembled Israelite
women, who lived to serve their men and served them
staunchly and without complaint. The stream, swollen with
melting snow from the mountains to the east, bounded and
tumbled between black, water-rounded rocks, and occasional
fish—she did not know their name, but she knew that they
carried their young in their mouths—glinted silverly near
the surface and tempted warriors to become fishermen. Wist-

fully she remembered Crete. Here, as there, the Goddess bedecked herself in Joseph-coated colors and pleaded for peace instead of war.

She passed the tent of Rizpah and felt a warmth of pity for the woman who had risked Saul's rage and Goliath's rape to stay in the camp, and now, in the opening to her tent, smiled dimly and nodded to Ahinoam. Her eyes were red, her cheeks were streaked with kohl. She did not look as if she had slept for several nights.

"How is it with Saul?" Ahinoam asked.

"His demon has fled before David's harp. Now he must face Goliath."

"He will be too weak. He must find a champion to fight in his place. But not Jonathan."

Ahinoam walked boldly among the soldiers. She liked to watch them in the first light of dawn. Men of all ages, men of all trades, bricklayers, shepherds, farmers, potters, millers, many untrained, most of them following Saul in his endless wars less out of hatred for the Philistines, whom they scarcely understood, than out of loyalty to Saul, who fought because Samuel commanded him to destroy the "pagan idolaters" and because, though born a farmer, he had become at last a fighter who knew no other art.

She liked to help the men prepare their breakfasts, for fighters needed more than the usual bread and cheese of farmers, and they fed on the countryside—the quail and the wild goats and the scaly fish (and hungered after the fish without scales and the wild boars which their religion forbade them to eat). She mended a goatskin tunic, she asked a bearded old patriarch who had been a friend of Samson about his great-grandchildren, and since Saul was not at hand to accuse her of sorcery, she healed a young man of the White Sickness with a simple laying on of hands.

The men, she knew, regarded her as an earthly Ashtoreth and paused in their tasks to watch her and wonder if, like the Lady, she had known a thousand lovers before she came to this land where women were stoned if they took a single lover. She smiled and nodded and asked about this man's child, that man's wound, and spoke of Israel and her victories under Saul. Not since Deborah, the Judge, had a woman evoked such adoration from an army.

"My lady, Goliath has returned. You must flee to Gibeah."
It was Caspir, the limping soldier from Michmash.

"I trust our men to rid us once and for all of that scourge."

He shook his head. "Saul is unwell. He is not the hero of
Jabesh-Gilead. Will my lady share my breakfast with me?
I netted a quail last night."

"No, Caspir, I am not hungry. But you are gracious to ask
me." (Quail turned her stomach; like the Lady of the Wild
Things, she loved birds and animals far too much to eat
them and lived entirely on vegetables; she was not in the
least like Alecto!) "Here, your fire is going out. Arrange the
sticks so—in a little pyramid. . . ."

A stench of sour wine and excrement drifted to her across
the stream. She had forgotten how silently Goliath and his
people could move in spite of their size. She forced herself
to turn and confront him, the single red eye, the red patches
of hair which bristled through his breastplate and greaves
and crested purple helmet and reminded her of a huge, two-
legged wolf in armor.

"The Queen of Honey has grown more delectable," he
said. "But the grape unplucked is devoured by birds or
shrivels into a raisin."

The Israelites had begun to gather around her in a de-
fensive circle. She suddenly realized that their wish to protect
her was not unmixed with suspicion. She, the legendary
queen from Caphtor, so the giant implied, had known him
before she came to Israel. Had she lain with him?

"Step back from the stream, my lady," warned Caspir.
"You are within range of his spear."

She was less afraid of his spear than his revelations. More
legends, more whispers. (*Not only does she come from
Caphtor, she knows Goliath. . . .*)

Let there be no mistake. She called in a voice as sweet and
poisonous as oleander, "The Giant of Caphtor has grown
more hideous with the years. His eye is as large as a squid's
and his honeyed words are spoken with a thick and drunken
tongue." Inwardly she shuddered lest he speak of her hidden
wings. Still, she did not turn from his stare.

He laughed, "The better to see you with," and moved
down the stream opposite the Israelite campfires and resumed
the boast she had heard in the night:

"Choose a man for yourselves, and let him come down to

me. If he is able to fight with me and kill me, then we will be your servants; but if I prevail against him and kill him, then you shall be our servants and serve us."

Himself beyond range of Israelite spears, he lifted his own spear—tipped with deadly iron like a battering ram—and hurled it across the stream. It lodged in the back of an Israelite, who had stooped to gather manna from a tamarisk bush. The spear was attached to a cord; before the others could reach and free their friend, Goliath yanked the cord, spear, and body through the stream and onto his own bank. Then, with a look so diabolical that it would have frozen a Night Stalker, he seized the corpse in his hands and tore the head from the trunk.

"Thus for Saul and Jonathan and the other mosquitoes of Israel," he boasted. "If you do not accept my challenge, I will leap this little rivulet you call a river and swat your king with my fist and crush his son with my boot and take his queen for my pleasure."

He laughed again and, having repeated his boast, knelt to drink from a quiet pond, protected from the mainstream by a ridge of stone and tree stumps. Ahinoam witnessed a curious sight, unnoticed, apparently, by the men. Momentarily Goliath saw his reflection in the pond. He shuddered and quickly stirred the waters to break the liquid mirror. He is appalled by his own ugliness, she recalled, and recalled, too, the tale that the Goddess had quarreled with the first Cyclopes because they had felled her trees and murdered her animals, and she had laid a curse of ugliness upon them: "You who see with two eyes and see no beauty in all of my creation, shall see with one eye, and ugliness shall stalk you to the end of your graceless days, and you shall be ugly even to each other and yourselves." And the Cyclopes, who had been like bad, undisciplined children, now became ruthless and crafty adults who warred with all other peoples, smashing what was built, crushing what was grown, cultivating oaths as poets cultivate epithets. There was even a poem among Ahinoam's people:

Dialogue

"Cyclops,
Red and squid-eyed,
Why do you plunder ships?"

"Because, kneeling to drink, I meet
Myself."

Understanding could be a curse for Ahinoam. To surmise
people's secrets meant to pity their pain. But she did not pity
Goliath, she hardened her heart against him for the sake of
Jonathan.

She turned quickly to leave the stream.

Goliath called after her, "I will come for you, Honey
Hair." No one had called her Honey Hair since she had left
her hive. Now the name seemed a desecration.

She turned and shouted back to him. "If my son were
well—"

"Ah, he must be a young man now. And comely like his
mother. I will enjoy breaking his back."

He wrenched a tree from the ground and cast it into the
stream. It seemed to please him to see the yellow flowers dis-
integrating in the frolicsome current.

"Water is for bathing as well as drinking. Or perhaps your
odor is your deadliest weapon," she said and, with dignity as
well as courage, turned her back on him and walked to
Jonathan's tent.

She was shocked to see him standing without support in
the door to the tent. His face was pale and thin from the
weight he had lost. He looked like a slender figurine of alabaster, woundingly beautiful, pathetically breakable. He was
Jonathan, the dreamer, instead of Jonathan, the warrior. He
was Jonathan, the boy who had fled to his tree house when
his father had scolded him for reading a scroll instead of
practicing with his bow. It came to her like the slap of a
wave that she who had lost a hundred lovers to hush-winged
death, that she who had lost a country and found a kingdom
only to lose its king, could not endure the loss of Jonathan.

"Jonathan, you should never have left your couch!" she
cried.

"That monster woke me with his threats. Just a few more
days and I'll be well enough to fight him."

He swayed in the door and she reached to steady him.
"Not if you rise too soon."

"Walk with me then," he said. "It will help me regain my
strength."

He put his arm around her shoulders—she felt his thinness

and thought of savory broths to plumpen him—and they began a slow inspection of the camp. The soldiers cheered when they saw him on his feet, and she heard them whisper among themselves.

"It's her healing magic again. 'Twas a fierce demon he fought."

"Without her he'd be dead."

"Soon he'll fight Goliath."

"You hear what they say?" he asked.

"Ignore them," she said with surprising vehemence. "If you were as strong as Saul in his prime, you still couldn't match that beast."

He looked like a little boy who had stubbed his toe. "You're not a warrior, Mama. Why do you think so little of my skill? I wouldn't let him touch me. He has the strength but I have the speed."

"He is swifter than you think. Remember, I knew him on Crete."

"But now he's old, and maybe tired like Father."

"If you fight him, he will win."

He shook his head. "Now you're being a sphinx. The men know you came from Crete, but what must I say when they ask me other questions? You have told me that you are a Siren. But how can you hear the sound which has not been made and see the sight which has not been seen? How can you look so young that you drive the Israelite matrons to dye their hair with henna, and the virgins to practice your walk and your voice and your enigmatic smile? Why do you keep such secrets from your own son?"

"My dear," she sighed, her hair a burst of sunflowers, her skin the pink flawless texture of the daffodils along the Philistine coast; an old woman who looked eternally young; a woman who would trade her youth to recover an old love. "We must each have secrets, you and I. Mine are those of age, yours of youth."

"Secrets are for strangers," he said. "But you are my mother."

"All men and women are strangers. Sometimes I think that the Celestial Vineyard is the place where strangeness falls away from us and we accept each other as we are, without the need to condemn or idealize."

"Must we wait so long?"

"Here's David," she cried with relief. "He'll take you back to your tent."

"I want you to take me," Jonathan said stubbornly. But already David had joined them and encircled Jonathan's shoulder with a powerful arm.

"I can walk alone," Jonathan protested.

"Hold still or you'll fall," said David. "I don't care if you are a prince. You're going to do what I say."

Covertly Ahinoam watched them as they accompanied her to the tent and observed the constraint which had come between them. She was neither misled nor displeased. She knew that unreasoning anger is often the other face of love.

"Stay with him," said Ahinoam, once in the tent. "I'll mix his drink. We don't want the fever to return. The demons are probably still in the vale."

David settled Jonathan on his couch, propped his head on a cushion, and summoned Mylas from his rug.

"Come and comfort your master," he said and, obeyed by the bear, he sat on the edge of the couch while Jonathan, silent, stroked Mylas' fur and tried to avoid David's look. Ahinoam smiled—how this boy took command with stubborn Jonathan!—and left the tent to prepare her son's potion from an herbal bag she had brought on her journey.

When she returned, David rose as if to leave her with Jonathan. "He wants to sleep, I think."

"He will sleep better with you in his tent."

"Will you, Jonathan?"

Jonathan was slow to answer. "Yes, David. If you sing to me first."

"I haven't a lyre with me. Shall I fetch one?"

"No. Just sing."

David sang with a rough, halting tenderness, and Ahinoam guessed that he was composing the song expressly for Jonathan.

Ibis

"Ibis,
Amber and alabaster:
In the green caverns of papyrus,
He cannot hear the dahabeah's prow
Sunder the Nile,
Nor the winds from Karnak,

> Freighted with sand and incense.
> But the caverns speak
> With little myriad voices:
> Scarab, lizard, and dragonfly
> Eddying pollen among the lotuses.
>
> What need has the amber bird
> For winds and rivers?"

Jonathan smiled and touched David on the shoulder. "Sometimes I don't understand your songs, but they ease my spirit."

Ahinoam restrained a protest. Understand! Why, the song was as clear as Goliath's mirror-pool. Like most Israelite poets, David couched his language in metaphors from nature, but it was clear to her—and certainly to her son—that Jonathan was the ibis and that he had no need to confront the winds and rivers of war because David had come to protect him.

David seized Jonathan's hand. "Why do you want to fight Goliath? You haven't a chance against him! Probably nobody in Israel has. It would settle nothing anyway, even if you killed him. Goliath's boast that he would let us depart is meaningless. He's not a seren, just a hired mercenary. The Philistines pay him with gold and women to fight for them. We would still have to fight Philistia."

"If I slew him, the Philistines might lose heart. Remember at Michmash how they panicked when Nathan and I pretended to be an army and took them by surprise in the night?"

"But you couldn't slay him."

"David, I have to fight Goliath. He's always been evil and he threatens my mother."

"You're speaking of fever dreams," said Ahinoam hastily, preferring that even David should not know the truths which she had told her son. "They are often lies."

"I'm not talking about a dream," said Jonathan, forgetting the reticence of half his life, forgetting the Israelite view of people with wings. "It's what you—"

Fortunately, Saul and Abner interrupted Jonathan's confession. Saul, though pale and gaunt, had temporarily mastered his demon and resumed control of the army.

"I am pleased to see my son improving so rapidly," he

said. "Our young David here is good for him, it seems. And you, Ahinoam. You too have helped to make him well."

"But not well enough to fight Goliath."

"Has my queen become my general?" he asked with gentle irony. He knew that she was intimately familiar with all of his battles, and he sometimes resented the fact that a woman who looked like one of the old Cretan queens languishing in a garden of blue lotuses should have a warrior's—indeed a general's—knowledge of war. Still, he sometimes forgot his resentment and addressed her as an equal.

"Your queen is whatever you choose," she said.

"The men are deserting by the hundred. They can face Philistines but not this hired horror."

Ahinoam shuddered. "I know. Someone must fight him, and soon."

"I will fight him," said Abner. She liked the man; loved him, in fact, as one might love a father or an uncle. When Saul was mad, Abner commanded the army with quiet and self-effacing skill. When Saul was well, Abner advised him in such a way that every decision seemed to belong to the king. Israel could not afford to lose such a man.

"How many times must I forbid you from such a folly?" said Saul. "Israel loves you as a second king, and I—" confession did not come easily to him—"I depend on your counsel and love you more than my brothers."

Jonathan pressed his father's hand. "The demons of fever are no respecters of war. First Goliath, then me. But I am much, much better, Father. Soon I can face Goliath."

"The demons have blessed you," said Saul. "Otherwise, not I nor all of my army could have kept you from battling that giant."

"You think I would lose?"

"He could lift you over his head with one hand and toss you across the stream. Even in my youth I doubt that I could have slain him. Do you want to join Nathan in Sheol?"

"At least I would have good company," said Jonathan with surprising bitterness.

"Such words are not worthy of the man who will succeed me as king of Israel. You should turn your thoughts to the mountains and not the Underworld."

"Forgive me, my father. The fever has left me with a

sharp tongue. I am sorry that you and my friend David should hear——"

"He has gone," said Ahinoam quietly.

"Where?" asked Saul with surprise. Musicians and armor-bearers did not as a rule leave his presence without permission.

"To meet Goliath, where else?"

Alone, in a ring of acacia trees, Ahinoam prayed to the Goddess:

> "Lady of the Wild Things,
> Harken to my prayer. . . .
> Send death to the deadly,
> Love to the lovely and loveless.
> I, Ahinoam, queen over Israel,
> Though an exile from my husband's tent,
> An affront to your fecundity,
> Offer to you
>
> My youth,
> My beauty,
> My life.
> I, Honey Hair,
> Sometime queen of green magic,
> Offer to you
> My sweet and eternal hope
> Of the Celestial Vineyard."

Chapter

SIX

When David left the tent, his intention was clear: to fight Goliath. His expectation was equally clear: he would die in the fight. But Jonathan was sick, Saul was weak, Abner was old and inexpendable, and none of the stalwarts of Israel, the victors of Michmash, had offered to meet the giant. It was not only his size; it was not only his savagery. It was his single balefully glaring eye which leagued him, in the Israelite mind, with Lilith, Night Stalkers, Walk-Behinders, and other supernatural being spewed out of Sheol by Yahweh's wrath. Such beings were not the figments of superstition; one of David's friends from Bethlehem had met a Lilith in a mountain cave and fled before she could lure and vampirize him; a couple from Gibeah had found a dwarf with horns in their baby's crib.

"Yahweh preserve me," he whispered, since Yahweh, whatever his limitations, was the lord of battles. Expressly against the god's commandments, he had sometimes worshipped the silver-tongued Ashtoreth, but perhaps the god would forget his apostasy and use him as a means to save his chosen people (and David's chosen person) from the Philistines.

Like all good shepherds, he was used to danger. He had fought with bears and lions, storms and floods, marauding Midianites on camels and local thieves on foot. Invariably he was terrified at first, since he lacked the blind, brute courage of his older and less intelligent brothers, but fear worked a curious chemistry in his body. He was young and middling in height, but now he felt as tall as Goliath. Furthermore, even though logic told him that the giant was unconquerable, he remembered that high-walled cities like Jericho had fallen to a motley band of wanderers out of the desert. It was as if his veins ran lava instead of blood.

Terror, then courage, then a cool and logical assessment of the problems at hand: such was the pattern in David; such his skill as a fighter. How could a boy fight a being twice his height, with bronze armor and iron weapons and a single-minded lust to kill and dismember? David himself owned neither weapons nor armor. He wore a tunic given to him by Jonathan, figured with bears and foxes, and the garment would bring him luck in the fight and companion him. But he must companion the tunic with suitable weapons.

"David," Ahinoam called. He paused to marvel at the speed and grace with which she overtook him. He had never seen sweat on her face. He had never seen dirt on her hands. She could survive the discomfort of a day-long ride on a donkey's back and look as if she were dressed to undress for a fertility rite. The scent of her was like sea spray and ambergris. Where other Israelite women, including Rizpah, muffled themselves in woolens against the heat and the heat of men's desire, she walked in silken transparencies like the wings of a dragonfly.

"You'll need weapons. Jonathan is sending you his armor by Saul."

"But how did he know—how did you know I meant to fight Goliath?"

"I saw it in your face. So did Jonathan. Surely you know by now that we can look into your heart. Jonathan wanted to stop you, but Saul prevented him and posted a guard outside his tent."

"Do you want to stop me?"

In the shadow of a tamarisk tree, her eyes looked gray and sad and ten thousand years too old for her bountiful body. As if she had seen the coming of the Sea Kings to Crete. The building of the great pyramids. The Hyksos invasion of Egypt . . .

She shook his hand. "David, David, you must see that Jonathan cannot fight. Or Saul. It has to be you. You have more power than you know."

"You think I can kill Goliath?"

"The oracles are silent of bells. Even the gods, perhaps, are undecided. You see, my dear, you come from a land which worships Yahweh, but you fight a people who worship Ashtoreth. And I, even I, am sometimes divided between them, the Lady of the Wild Things and the Lord of the Mountaintops. But I think that in all of Israel only you have a chance."

"Why, my lady?"

"Because you are beautiful and the Great Mother deplores the broken bird, the drowned dolphin. Because you fight for Jonathan, who is dear to Israel, which is dear to Yahweh. Because, for what it is worth, I will fight with you in my heart."

"The men say you brought green magic from Caphtor. The double magic of sea and forest." (He started to add: "They also say that you once had wings." But it would be like saying to one-armed Caspir, "They say that you once had another arm.") "Is it true, my lady?"

"Magic is knowing the moods of the gods. Which to please and how. Perhaps I have magic with Ashtoreth. Her moods are like the tides or the phases of the moon. She is a goddess but also a woman; a woman but also a mother. Unpredictable but in the end compassionate. With Yahweh, who knows? Being a local god, he is readily offended. I will leave it to Saul to woo his favor."

"Do you think he will listen?" Supported by Rizpah, Saul had overtaken them. "I have it from Samuel himself that Yahweh has gone from me." He turned to address David. "My son, your music has brought me peace. I do not ask that you give your life as well."

His great height and immensely broad shoulders bespoke a time when he had been king in truth, though fevers and madness had wracked him to a shell which even his robes could not conceal. He was old, proud, dying Jerusalem, gray of wall and tower, haggard from many winters, a ghost instead of a presence, but still defended by the Jebusites.

"For a long time I kept my father's sheep," said David. "Once a lion came after them and carried off a lamb. I went after him and smote him and delivered it out of his mouth, and I caught him by the beard and slew him."

Saul shook his head. "Your confidence is admirable, but Goliath could kill a dozen lions."

"The Lord that delivered me out of the paws of the lion will deliver me from Goliath." The words did not come easily to him; though born of that pious tribe, the Benjamites, he did not understand his god. But he wished to give Saul a reason to let him fight.

"Go then and the Lord be with you. But first we must find you some armor." He signaled to the guard in front of Jonathan's tent: "Bring my son's armor and weapons. All of it so that David may take a choice."

Sword, helmet of brass, and coat of mail: how could he bear such weight and wield such a weapon, he who had always fought with his hands or at most with a staff?

"They won't fit him, Saul," said Ahinoam. "Jonathan is taller and slimmer."

"What do you know of such things?" Saul asked wearily.

"Was I not with you at Jabesh-Gilead?"

(She is robed in chrysanthemums. Daisies spring when she walks and caresses the earth. And yet she speaks like a warrior. . . .)

Saul gave a little sigh. "Yes, Ahinoam. You were with me

then, and now." He moved as if to touch and perhaps embrace her but, remembering Rizpah, dropped his arms to his side.

(*He is still in love with her, but Rizpah is comfortable, and the old need comfort more than passion. It is hard for advancing age to confront eternal youth.*)

"I've never worn armor before," said David. He lifted the sword and wished for a shepherd's staff. ("When I am well, I will teach you to use a sword," Jonathan had said. "When I am well . . ."). "No, my lord, I must fight him without armor."

Saul spoke with puzzlement. "But these things belong to Jonathan. The best in Israel next to mine."

"I would feel as if I were walking on the bottom of the sea. Goliath would trample me into the ground and hang Jonathan's armor, together with my head, on the walls of Beth-Shan."

"What do you know about the sea?" The question was almost an accusation.

"Only what I have dreamed. I have never seen the sea."

Ahinoam took Saul's hand. "Dreams are often warnings. Trust him, my dear." Saul removed his hand and pain, like a seagull's shadow, fleetingly crossed her face. Thus did goddesses grieve beneath their masks.

Rizpah, standing apart from them, smiled her human and pathetic smile. "My father was once a shepherd. He was also a fearsome fighter. Let David do as he chooses, my lord."

"How do you want to fight him?" Saul demanded.

"The only way I know." He returned the armor to Saul. "Please tell Jonathan that he has honored me with his offer. I will bring him the head of Goliath."

Ahinoam embraced him as if he were Jonathan. "My second son, come back to me in triumph."

"I love your son," he said. "It's only for him and you that I can do this thing."

"And for you, we say, 'In the midst of battle, *remember the sea.*'"

Rizpah shyly patted his shoulder; her hand was plump and heavily jeweled with rings of gold and garnet; her robe a garish mingling of red and orange. Beside Ahinoam she looked like a painted and aging whore instead of a king's concubine; pathetic and therefore lovable.

"My son, may Yahweh go with you," said Saul, an old man remembering youth.

"Now I must get my sling."

He went to look for his brothers and found them chatting with a young Philistine across the stream. After a month of waiting to join battle, a camaraderie had grown between the two armies, and, enjoying the benefits of a common language, Philistine chattered with Israelite about the respective merits of Yahweh and Ashtoreth; the hills and the sea coast; sleeping under the sky or under a tent.

"We worship Ashtoreth too," Eliab was saying, "so long as Samuel isn't around."

"You don't know how to worship her properly," said a Philistine youth. "You keep your robes on."

"We have heard that your priests and priestesses disrobe and couple before your very eyes," Eliab said, with the look of a hungry man.

"And we participate. Men and women, men and men, women and women. Take your pick, so long as you lie with someone you truly love. Why do you think our fields are fertile in spite of the winds from the sea? Because we please Ashtoreth, that's why."

"We can't even enjoy a woman in private—not even a *wife*—for three days before a battle. And as for a man lying with a man, why, Yahweh would smite them both with a thunderbolt or turn them to pillars of salt!"

The Philistine grinned and clapped a passing friend on the back. "He sounds like a grouchy old god. He'd do a lot of smiting in Philistia. Sin and retribution and pride. We don't think about such things. Yahweh says don't. The Lady says do. I expect she will give us the victory, what with Goliath on our side."

"He smells. Even across the stream."

"And steals and rapes. But he sleeps a lot. And he's better than a hundred chariots. And you without a champion to go up against him."

"No," said David quietly.

"David!" Eliab cried. They had not even met since David became the king's armorbearer, and the big brother was no longer the big man of the family.

"No what?"

"No. We're no longer without a champion. I am going to fight Goliath."

Eliab and Ozem and Nethanel—and the Philistine across the stream—looked at David as if they did not know whether to greet him as a hero or a fool. In Bethlehem, as the youngest member of the family, he had been a shepherd when his brothers went to war. Now, by the grace of Yahweh, he was the king's armorbearer; and furthermore, in place of Jonathan, he was preparing to fight Goliath. David was tempted to swagger and play the hero, but a fight in behalf of Jonathan was not an occasion for pride.

"I've come for my sling," he said.

The three brothers gaped at him as if they had not heard his request. Finally Eliab said:

"You may use my sword." It was his one precious possession.

David shook his head. Then, impulsively, he hugged his brothers in turn and was deeply touched to find tears on Eliab's face, and to hear Nethanel stifle a sob. None of Jesse's sons could read or write except David; they were fighters and herdsmen, with neither learning nor wisdom nor wit. But they were good young men, devout in their worship of Yahweh, and sometimes David envied their simplicity.

They stared after him and shook their heads as he walked toward Jonathan's tent.

He found the prince on his couch, flushed with the remnants of fever and drenched with sweat. David sat beside him and pushed him gently onto his back. Jonathan had the body of a runner, not a wrestler; smooth and slim instead of knotted with muscles. His face showed lines of pain, but he was singularly beautiful even in his illness; inhumanly beautiful, like his mother.

"You're going to fight him?"

"Yes."

"I should be the one."

"And so you will, Jonathan. You will fight through me."

Quite unintentionally, and so quickly that Jonathan could neither respond nor refuse, he bent and kissed the fevered cheek. He rose and fled from the tent, without looking behind him till Jonathan called his name, once, softly.

"David."

The word would be his armor.

When he returned to Saul and Ahinoam, he was still wearing Jonathan's tunic, with two additions—a small sack
suspended from his shoulder and a sling in his hand. The
usual Israelite sling was no more than two narrow strips of
leather sewn together at one end into a small pouch for
holding a stone. One end the slinger held; the other he tied
to his wrist; and he flung the stone with sufficient force to
stop a bear or a lion but not a giant. David wisely preferred
an Assyrian sling, a gift from a cousin who had fought as a
mercenary for the Wolves of the North. Both sturdier and
deadlier than the Israelite sling, it was a single strip attached
to a leather cup. He would hold the strip toward the middle,
whirl the sling, and then, with a slight twist of the wrist,
release the stone with the speed, force, and accuracy of long
and intensive practice. Such a missile could not pierce armor,
but it could strike the forehead, the forearm, the ankle below
the greaves, and wound or even kill. In Assyria, so he was
told, it was the usual practice to wound and then, with the
foe either limping in pain or stretched on the ground, make
the kill with a sword.

Swordless David knelt beside the stream and gathered five
smooth stones, drying and weighing each in his hand before
he placed it in his pouch. Jagged stones would have been
more wounding, but smooth ones were more predictable in
their flight and, ultimately, more lethal.

"A slingshot!" cried Saul. "Why, that's a child's toy. You
forget you're no longer a shepherd boy."

"The Assyrians never fight without their slingers," David
reminded the king. He was more knowledgeable about Assyrian armies than about his father's herd. Also, Egyptian,
Edomite, Ammonite, and Midianite, to say nothing of Philistine. "Their missiles are nothing more than baked clay pellets,
and yet they're conquering the Babylonians. But river stones
are harder and deadlier. We say in Bethlehem that a Ben-
jamite can sling a stone at a hare and catch him as he jumps."

Saul shrugged with weary resignation. "Well, then, fight
your giant. I have no wish to watch the slaughter." He turned
and stalked toward his tent, to "cleanse his robe," according
to an old expression, of the ill-omened affair. Rizpah, with
a wistful look at David and the ghost of a smile, followed
her lord. Ahinoam remained with David.

"If your river stones fail," she said, "use this. It is small but very hard. Such stones hold the Lady's magic." She gave him Jonathan's bee-shaped tourmaline.

He fondled it carefully and judged its weight. Too light, he thought, but I must please her because she is sad, she and Jonathan. They expect me to die.

"And David, remember the sea."

He did not question the cryptic advice, but knelt and kissed her hand. (Such small hands for one so ripe. Hands like butterflies. To press them would be to wound them. How white they are! Are they covered with magic dust like a butterfly wing?)

He rose and looked into her eyes and wanted to cry like a little boy and be held and comforted by this goddess, this queen, this woman who seemed to him the Great Mother, the universal comforter.

"Ask Jonathan to wish me well," he said.

"May the Lady walk with both of you, and may the two of you soon walk together." She smoothed his ruffled hair and the gesture seemed strangely poignant at such a time; a trifle yet touching. "I am going to watch your victory."

"Nobody else is going to watch me," he said. "They think I'm a mosquito attacking an elephant. Did you ever hear such a silence?"

"Look around you," she said. "It is the silence of watchfulness."

They might have been turned into salt, these Israelites, like Lot's unfortunate wife. No one stirred a fire, no one ate, no one polished a blade or hammered a tent peg; the army physician had dropped his herbal bag; one-armed Caspir knelt beside his blanket and looked to Ahinoam with wordless and worshipful sympathy; and in that hushed expectancy David could read man's eternal hope that, while kingdoms rise and fall, while chaos coalesces into gods and worlds, and then reclaims them, miracles remain, magic endures, sometimes the small prevail, the large are devoured by the dust and the worm.

Across the stream the Philistines watched him with an equal hush. A curious division showed in their shaven faces. Goliath fought in their place; Goliath could win the war for them. But they clearly despised the giant and admired the lad who dared to fight him. What had Ahinoam said? "The Philistines are not a wicked race. They are dreamers and

artists who are forced to bear arms by ambitious lords." If
he were king, he would try to make peace with them. If he
were king . . . It suddenly seemed to him that to be the king
of Israel was the highest dream he could dream. Except to
be loved by Jonathan. Thus did the several Davids war in
the single boy.

He knelt and discarded his sandals—his tough feet, so he
thought, needed no protection—and waded into the stream.
But every nerve was sensitized to the point of pain. He felt
the rocks like nettles . . . the chill of the water . . . a fish
against his ankle. He stumbled and fell to his knees and the
water slapped his face; rose and climbed the bank and stared
at the staring faces of ten thousand men.

He stood in a meadow of chrysanthemums. Beyond him
lay the flowerlike tents of the Philistines, their owners standing in groups to watch the fight, helmeted with their purple
plumes, holding their iron-tipped spears; expectant of victory,
but—hesitant? Doubting their own redoubtable champion?
Remembering, perhaps, Jonathan at Michmash. Remembering certainly the wrath of Yahweh when they stole his Ark.
Warriors, these men, but preferring peace. Seashore and sea-
grapes . . . gardens where mulberry trees delighted the bee
and the wasp . . . white palaces with crimson columns . . .
dreamers and artists.

Goliath, guarded by his armorbearer, pretended to drowse
beneath a terebinth tree. His jaw hung slack; his head lolled
on his shoulder; he looked more absurd than threatening.

But the single eye fluttered and watched. . . .

"All right, Big Mouth," David shouted. "You've got your
champion."

Goliath stared first at David and then over his head, probably taking the boy for an armorbearer to a seasoned warrior, Abner or even Saul.

"Get up, One Eye, or I'll smite you where you sit!"

Goliath recognized his adversary and began to laugh. His
laughter resembled the yelp of hyenas around a corpse.

"Am I a dog that you come to me with a sling? Cursed be
your Yahweh that he can't find a champion more worthy of
me. I will give your flesh to the vultures and the lions."

"You've cursed the wrong god," cried David, secretly wishing that the giant had cursed the Lady and alerted her to the
plight of a shepherd boy. "It was Yahweh who sent a pesti-

lence on the Philistines when they stole his Ark. And who do you think it was who opened the Red Sea and—" what *was* another miracle to dismay a giant?—"afflicted Pharaoh with a thousand boils?"

Goliath yawned and scratched his back against the tree. "Come closer, mosquito. I can hardly hear you buzz." He was still out of David's range, and the closer David approached him, the hillier grew the ground, the harder to climb and cast with accuracy.

"Like Sheol I'll come to you!" cried David. "I won't take another step till you leave your tree."

Ahinoam's voice rang silkenly over the stream to Goliath. "I have heard," she said, "that your mother was a Gorgon and your father a squid instead of a god. The combination is unfortunate, to say the least. You win your battles by ugliness, not by prowess. Like a Gorgon's head, the sight of you turns men to stone. Or perhaps your odor overpowers their senses. Once you threatened to break the back of my son Jonathan. Now you threaten his friend David. Either rise and meet him or skulk away to your brothers in high-walled Gath."

Goliath erupted to his feet. A confusion of flesh and armor became a single and formidable being. The absurdity became a killer. He wore a brass helmet and a coat of mail; the staff of his iron-tipped spear was as large as a weaver's beam. Six hundred shekels it must have weighed. His striding feet were an earthquake, the terebinth tree shed leaves on the jungle of his hair. He smelled like a beached and rotting whale. Even David, whose nostrils were used to sheep dung and the blood of slaughtered lambs, choked and held his breath.

Goliath seized his shield from his armorbearer and shoved the boy to the ground.

"Be quicker, brat," he snarled.

Indeed, the "brat" was too slow. Goliath had come within range of David's sling; he did not have time to raise his shield. By now David had obliterated all distractions, sounds, sights, and scents from his mind. His body obeyed him instantly and automatically; his sling whistled in an arc beside him; he twisted his wrist with the delicacy and deftness of a cutpurse; the stone wooshed through the air . . . fast . . . straight . . . and struck the giant directly above his eye.

Such a shot would have crushed the skull of a normal man. Goliath touched his head, more in surprise than pain. He had not expected the blow. The mosquito had a sting. He had taken the stone a hundred paces from David; he came at the boy like a wind devil out of the hills.

David's arm became a continuous arc; stone followed stone, only to strike the impenetrable shield and fall uselessly to the ground. Four shots; four useless hits; and the giant engulfed him like a tidal wave, snatched his stream-wet arm but slipped and caught him by the edge of his tunic; flung him into the air like a bit of flotsam, a lost and battered oar.

He could have killed me at once with his spear, thought David. He wishes to play with me. I am the minnow to his shark. At least I shall nip his fins before he devours me.

(*"And David . . . remember the sea. . . ."*)

He who had never swum except in rivers, never in the salty expanses of the Great Green Sea, remembered that the sea supports as well as drowns and gave himself willingly to the currents of the air. I am a dolphin, he thought. A tarpon . . . a flying fish . . . the young Dagon, swift to ride the waves. And when I alight on the ground I will not be tense and broken but ready to rise again and climb, if necessary, the buoyant air.

He fell in a clump of wild chrysanthemums. The flowers softened his fall; relaxed and agile, he felt as if he had floated to the bottom of the sea. He felt an overwhelming urge to dream among the chrysanthemums. Sea anemones . . . blue currents laving his tired limbs . . . dolphins to ease and protect him.

Goliath jolted him out of his deadly lassitude. Here was the shark. Here was the killer. He must get to his feet and search for other stones. He had turned the air into sea and softened his fall, but he must not drown.

Goliath raised his foot. *He is going to fulfill his threat. He is going to trample me. I can roll. I can rise, but where can I flee to escape his crushing boot?* Before he had fought the lion, he had dreaded to lose the light of the sun, the embrace of virgins, the power of music, the solitary hill beneath the harvest moon. He had grieved until wrath had made him strong. Now, he was more than a sweet-singing shepherd boy, he was armorbearer to Saul, friend to the son of Saul. *Jona-*

*than, Jonathan, must I await you in Sheol, where dust mingles
with dust and shadows may meet but never touch?*

Why did the raised boot not complete its descent? Why
did the monster freeze in his final, fatal blow? Why did confusion, yes, and even fear wrinkle the glaring eye? (*Jonathan's
tent . . . the shifting shapes in his arms . . . the sheep . . . the
Nereid . . . the green magic of Caphtor . . . and the exquisite
gift of time . . .*) They have lent me their magic, he thought,
Ahinoam and Jonathan. Their metamorphoses. I am chang-
ing before Goliath's eye. Who can say what horror he sees in
my place? What does he fear the most? The sight of his own
face. *He sees me as his own reflection in a stream.*

"I will not die!" The words were a trumpet call.

He fitted his last stone, Jonathan's tourmaline, into his
sling and somehow, propped on his other arm, flung the
stone awkwardly upward and toward the bewildered eye.

I have missed, he thought, or done him no harm with so
light a shot. He stands above me frozen like an Assyrian
statue. Stone; stony and heartless. No welt has appeared on
his brow. His boot will complete its descent and grind me
into the flowers.

The earth exulted with Goliath's fall.

Chapter
SEVEN

David approached the entrance to Jonathan's tent, waving
the grisly relic of his triumph. He had forgotten to recover
his sandals; his hair was a dusty whirlwind atop his head.
His hands and arms dripped gore. Warriors clamored around
him to beg for a lock of Goliath's hair, or his spear, or his
sword, or the red eye which, though embedded with Jonathan's tourmaline, still glared wickedly from the severed head.
His brothers chanted his name like a conjuration: "David,
David, David . . ."

"It is Samson come again!"

"Beware of Delilahs, little brother!"

"You've put them to route, the whole idolatrous army! They're not even taking their tents."

Why, even the king was clapping him on the shoulder and shouting, "Armorbearer no more! I'll make you the captain of a thousand men. The youngest in all of Israel!"

"Jonathan," he cried, exploding into the tent without even answering Saul. "You won't have to fight Goliath!" I am drunk, he thought, of pomegranate wine. I have taken a virgin or worshipped the Lady at one of her harvest festivals. Now is the triumph of triumphs. Now I have come to Jonathan to give him the victory, for he has fought with me and through me, and he is truly the victor.

Jonathan raised his head and stared at him with blank, unblinking eyes. He parted his lips as if he wished to speak, but succumbed to a wave of nausea, repeated and sudden; he retched and gasped and crouched like a sick old man.

Yahweh preserve me, thought David. Insensitive brat that I am, I have brought a Cyclops' head to an ailing prince who despises war and refuses to kill a bee. He backed out of the tent and heaved the head into the groping hands of the soldiers. They would doubtless impale it on a stake and parade it up and down the stream before the few Philistines who had not yet fled toward the sea.

He waded into the stream and, using sand from the bank, carefully washed the blood from his arms and hands. Fortunately, his tunic, the gift from Jonathan, was free of blood. Cleansed of gore if not of grime, he returned to the prince's tent with hesitant steps.

Ahinoam and Saul had joined their son. "You are not to blame," she whispered to David. "Whatever demons torture him now, you will know how to exorcise them."

She looked as young as her daughter Michal, but her wise sad eyes bespoke another age and other lands; poets had sung her, kings had loved her to their destruction. ("Pomegranates are my lady's breasts, a hyacinth her hair ..." He would write a psalm to her; he too would have loved her except for Jonathan.)

"Come, Saul. Leave them together. Too many people will weary Jonathan. It is David's right to be with him now."

"If David could play a psalm of victory ..."

"Another time." She led him from the tent.

David sat on the edge of Jonathan's couch and tried to ignore the babble of voices beyond the goatskin walls.

'Still angry with me. little friend?"

Jonathan was taller by half a head than David, but David sometimes thought of him as a little boy: his tent, for example, with the carved animals and the painted blocks. It was almost as if obeying his father and becoming a fine warrior even though he hated to fight, he had resolutely held to a part of his life when he had been neither warrior nor hero but simply a child with toys.

Jonathan shook his head. "I was never angry with you." The yellow hair, uncombed for days, tumbled over his eyes and gave him the look of his own rumpled bear.

David took his hand. "I shouldn't have shown you the head. It's no wonder it made you sick."

"I've been fighting for my father since I was fourteen. I'm used to such sights."

'Then why were you sick?" demanded David. He was learning to exercise subtlety with Saul, but Jonathan and Ahinoam could read his heart. He must not evade them, though Jonathan evaded him. He must ask whatever questions troubled his heart, and Jonathan troubled him more than Goliath.

"Because you might have been killed. Because you had saved my life."

"Do you mean you feel you owe me a debt of gratitude, and that's a burden to you?" He knew that among the Midianites and certain other peoples a man whose life had been saved became the servant of his savior.

"It wasn't that I felt a debt. I don't know what I felt."

"You were angry with me even before I fought Goliath, weren't you?" David asked, trying to follow the intricacies of Jonathan's heart. It was a heart whose innocence was baffling and labyrinthine. "I didn't know why, but I knew you were. Maybe you got sick because you were ashamed of yourself for not having had a reason. When I brought you the head, it wasn't that I shocked you, it was that you knew I was—I was —' eloquent David struggled for words—"not somebody to be angry with."

"Oh, David, you don't understand at all."

He placed his hands on Jonathan's shoulders and wondered if he should shake him or hug him. "One thing I do understand is that you would have killed Goliath for me if I had been sick."

"I would have died for you," said Jonathan. "And given up my hope of the Celestial Vineyard."

David hugged him against his breast. Whatever shadows had fallen between them dissipated like the darkness in a tent at sunrise. But the prince felt frail and chilled, though the tent was warm from the midday sun.

"Shall I get you a robe?" asked David.

"No, not yet. You be my blanket. Will you sing to me?"

"I can't sing and be a blanket at the same time." He did not want to sing; he wanted to warm the prince with his love.

"Sing first and then—"

"About what?"

"Your songs are usually about the valleys and the pastures of Israel. Can you sing about the sea?"

"I don't know. I've never seen it and I didn't think you had either. The Philistines have always been in the way."

"I've seen it," said Jonathan. "Many times. Perhaps Ashtoreth will put the words into your mouth. You know, she is the guardian of sailors as well as lovers. Poseidon raises the waves and she becalms them."

"But our god is Yahweh."

"Oh, him. He's all very well in a battle. But not in a—in the kind of song I want to hear." It was arrant heresy, the prince of Israel scorning the national god of the Israelites, but David was neither surprised nor shocked. Only the very young or the very old of Israel singlemindedly worshipped Yahweh. David's own pantheon included the Israelite Yahweh, whom he invoked to protect his flocks, the Philistine Ashtoreth, whom he entreated to send him comely and compliant maidens, and the Midianite Sin, who, though a moon god, seemed to be good for luck in general. He excluded the fat old Baals who clamored for sacrifices of cattle to plumpen their bellies.

David wished for his harp, but the Goddess whispered a song about the sea and, of course, about Jonathan, and his voice was sweet and unfaltering:

"I saw him rising from the sea,
Dagon with starfish tangled in his hair
And eyes like chrysolites.

'Come play with me, come play with me,' he called,
'And we will gather conchs and cockleshells!'
But liquid fields are cold;
The shark, I thought,
Will cast strange shadows at my feet.
'Tomorrow,' I said,
'Tomorrow we will gather cockleshells.'
And Dagon laughed,
Slipping with dolphin-ease between the waves.
I saw the foam possess his tangled hair.
But first he said:
'Does dust know how to play?' "

"I was the speaker, wasn't I?" said Jonathan. "And of course you were Dagon. But he's the national god of the Philistines, and some of his images are gross and ugly, with a scaly fish's tail. That's not you at all."

"That's not the Dagon I mean. There's a young Dagon, too, who likes to play with the dolphins."

"On Caphtor we called him Palaemon. But how do you know so much about the sea?"

"I expect Ashtoreth put the thoughts in my brain."

"Ashtoreth or my mother."

"Sometimes I think they are one and the same. Both of them helped me in my fight against Goliath."

"I know. David, why do you always sing about me?"

"Because I love you."

He had never said such words, not to the comeliest virgin he had ever kissed, not even to his mother. Now he had said them to a man, though one of the gods they worshipped had presumably destroyed Sodom because its men did not always love its women. He felt as if he should blush with shame or explain that he meant only that he loved Jonathan like a brother. But he felt more pride than shame, and he did not love Jonathan like a brother.

(His father had once accused him of lacking a sense of sin. "Where would Abraham have been if he hadn't repented his sins?" Jesse had asked in one of his more asinine moods. David had answered without hesitation. "A prince of Egypt with twenty concubines and a golden calf in his garden.")

Now it was Jonathan's turn to touch instead of talk; he touched David's cheek with a tentative hand. A butterfly hand? No, there was nothing feminine in his touch. It did not seem to David that only then did they embrace as more than friends; it seemed to him that there had never been a time when they were less than lovers. Arm in arm they had crossed impassable deserts; side by side they had sailed impossible seas, farther than Sheba or Punt; beyond the edge of the world! Other lands had known them; in other times they had loved and shared the throne; the high-breasted Lady of Crete, twining snakes in her hands, had smiled beneficence on them; they were as young and as old as the pyramids.

"I know a secret place," said Jonathan. "Not like here, in the middle of an army."

"Is it far?"

"As far as Ophir. As close as today."

"Are you strong enough?"

"You will be my wings."

"I am taking the prince for a walk," he said to the guard outside the tent. "He must recover his strength. He can hardly stand by himself."

The guard, a young farmer with thick, callused hands, looked at David with adoration—the killer of Goliath!—and at Jonathan with admiration—the prince of Israel! David liked him for liking Jonathan.

"No danger now," the guard cried. "Not a Philistine in sight! Take good care of the prince, though, David. Goliath's brothers may come this way."

They followed the wildly meandering course of the stream. Oleanders, clustered with red blossoms, dipped their tapering fingerlike leaves into the water.

"Are we like that?" Jonathan asked his friend.

"Like what?"

"Oleanders. The leaves are smooth and straight, but the sap is poisonous."

For answer, David led him away from the stream and into a meadow of wild flowers and totter grass.

Jonathan fell to his knees and touched the earth in silent communication with her green children. "On Crete," he said, "the gods used to dance in dells like this, till they fled to the sky or under the sea."

Plucking an armful of yellow parsley flowers like little shields, David handed them to Jonathan.

"You're like these."

"Frail, do you mean?"

"Modest, valorous, and beautiful! Except your hair makes them pale in comparison."

The yellow flowers were mirrored in Jonathan's eyes, stars in green firmaments. He was more than human, of course. Perhaps he was an angel or a star god. But now he had come to earth, and it was the proof of his power that he should deserve but never demand worship.

Jonathan cradled the flowers in his arms. "We must give them to the stream. It's been a kind stream to make this vale so fruitful for us. Not even Goliath could spoil it." It seemed as if the flowers, spun in the clear waters, were speaking to the stream, and the stream was rumbling an answer about his journey from the mountains which he loved for their snow and into the lowlands which he loved because they frolicked with chrysanthemums and anemones, poppies, and purple catchflies; about David and Jonathan and how he loved them too because they had given him flowers, when other men drank him or washed in him and never thought of a gift.

"Here," said Jonathan, pausing and pointing excitedly to an oak tree which had probably been old when Abraham was young. Unlike the terebinth oracle, however, this tree luxuriated with fresh green foliage and offered the climbers notches up the trunk and into the green fastnesses, which twinkled with sunlit sparrows building nests. David loved them because, in spite of their tiny, colorless bodies, they were ready to fight an eagle or a wolf. They, too, must face their Goliaths.

It was rare to find so enormous a growth in Israel, where shrubs passed for trees and whose deserts outnumbered its forests.

"You won't make it up the trunk," said David. "You've been sick and there's nothing in your stomach."

"I will if you give me a push. I had a lot of practice when I was a boy. My parents would come here to Elah in the spring—we brought a tent to sleep in—but Michal and I built a house in this tree. I must have been ten at the time." He paused and said with surprise, "I was happy then. It was before Rizpah came." He looked searchingly into David's face. "It's come back, you know."

"What, Jonathan?"

"Feeling ten and happy."

"Those things never go away. They just hide until somebody uncovers them." David himself had been a happy boy
and a happy, if sometimes restless, youth. He had liked his
brothers; he had loved his parents, however foolish their ways;
and always, among the solitary hills, he could compose a
psalm or plan a battle. Still, he knew how it must have been
for Jonathan, who had to be a prince and command a thousand men and please a well-intentioned but misunderstanding
father whom he truly loved and, worst of all, endure his
mother's shame and recognize Rizpah in her place at court.

"Ten was hidden in me all this time, till you uncovered it,
like a toy—like a clay cart pulled by a donkey—which a
child played with before the Flood."

"Climb," said David, pushing him up the trunk, "we'll un-
cover it together," and soon they were in the house, which
Jonathan and Michal had built to withstand many weathers:
round-built, constructed of limb and clay laboriously carried
from the ground, with large windows, so that the wind could
sweep through them without wrecking the walls. The thatched
roof had departed with forgotten winters, but the single room
had held tenaciously to its furnishings: a portable hearth, a
three-legged stool, a drinking cup with a handle like a snake.

"The couch is gone," said Jonathan as if he were lamenting
a lost friend. "Its feet were the paws of a bear. I carved them
myself from cedar wood."

"But the floor is a couch; it's soft with leaves."

"We used to play that we were king and queen," said
Jonathan, "and this was our summer palace, where we got
away from the cares of the capital. The sparrows were our
subjects. You see, they're still here. Do you like sparrows,
David?"

"Better than phoenixes!"

"So do I. Their feathers are dull and their voices plain, but
they generally find something to sing about."

"They're just talking, Jonathan," said David, the musician,
"but I expect they find a lot of interesting things to say." A
sudden sadness chilled him like the trickle of air from a deep
well. Happiness is a sparrow, he thought, tenacious but brief
and frail. He knew that his future would shrill with clashing
eagles, with too many loves and loyalties and treacheries, and
that he would never again be a simple shepherd or an armorbearer who could climb a tree with Jonathan.

"You'll be a king one day, Jonathan. And doubtless you'll marry a princess from Egypt and forget all about me."

"You know I will never marry, David."

"Why not? It'll be a marriage of state. You don't have to love the princess. You want a son, don't you?"

"Twins," said Jonathan. "With red hair. But wanting isn't enough. At least I have my little brother, Ishbaal. Saul ignores him, so I have a chance to act like a father. Do you have to marry?" The question held its own wistful answer. An unmarried adult Israelite was as rare as manna after the hot melting sun of noon.

"I expect I shall. But it will have nothing to do with what I feel for you."

"Then you should marry my sister Michal. She's already in love with you, and she could help you with my father. He never seems to get angry with her. What's more you could make her happy. You wouldn't want my other sister, Merab. She's a scold."

"I don't want to marry anyone for a long time," said David.

Jonathan took his hand and spread the fingers—the large strong fingers of a shepherd—and smiled as he looked into the palm. "You had better start soon. If I'm counting right, I see nine wives and eighteen concubines in your future." He turned suddenly serious. "And I think I see an army . . . a war . . . and a throne."

"And you're with me?"

"Part of the way. Then we're separated. Then—I don't know."

"You see death, don't you?" David persisted.

"Not yours, David. I see many years for you."

"Yours then?"

"Who believes in palmistry anyway, except the Babylonians?"

"And the Babylonians are being swallowed up by the Assyrians, who don't believe in anything." He patted Jonathan's shoulder. "Rest now," he said. "Lie down on the leaves. I think you'll find them more comfortable than your lost couch."

Jonathan obeyed the command, but with a curious resignation, like a soldier going to a war from which he will never return. He looked at David with wide, solemn eyes.

David knelt beside him and kissed his cheek.

"It is the sin of Sodom," said Jonathan, still as a fallen image.

"Who says such a ridiculous thing?"

"My father. Samuel. Everybody except my mother and you."

"And who do you love best in the world?"

"You first. Then my mother."

"Well then, listen to us. A sin is when you hurt people. Are you afraid I'm going to hurt you?"

"I could never be afraid of you, David. It seemed I was always afraid until you came, though I couldn't admit it. At Michmash when Nathan and I attacked the Philistines, I was terrified, but I had to be strong for him. And because of my father."

"And I was terrified of Goliath. It was that single eye, I think. It never blinked. It just stared and stared and almost hypnotized me. What is courage without fear? It's nothing but foolhardiness. We're not fools, either of us."

For answer, Jonathan smiled and opened his arms, and David remembered watching Ahinoam, alone in a forest glade, open her arms to Ashtoreth and pray that the lovely and the loveless should find love. He entered Jonathan's embrace and seemed at last to know the fulness of the sea, which had tantalized him with fitful flickers, an image, a scent, some words in a song; for he entered a world where dolphins snorted in leaping multitudes and Sirens combed their tresses with combs of coral; and then they were under the sea, he and Jonathan, and the leaves of the oak tree were fathoms of cushioning water, and they swam into a cave where clumsy, amiable crabs brought gifts of amber between their pincers and a friendly octopus arranged them a couch of sea-weed and sea anemones.

Jonathan held him with a wild urgency, meeting mood for mood, making of touch a language more articulate than song, and in that ancient oak tree the eternal Ashtoreth was honored more richly than by prayer or sacrifice. . . .

"Sleep now, Jonathan, and I'll keep watch."

" 'Yea, though I walk through the valley of the shadow of death, I will fear no evil; for thou art with me. . . .' You wrote that, David, didn't you?"

"Yes, Jonathan. In a way, I wrote it for you." He had

written a song which men would always sing, in the valley or
on the mountaintop. He had fought and killed a giant. He
had liked a hundred girls and he knew that he would love a
score of women, a little, for a little while, and beget children
beyond number, but that he would never love anyone, neither
man nor woman, as he loved Jonathan. . . .

"I will find you food while you sleep."

"Don't leave me, David."

"Not until you sleep."

David watched the golden lashes extinguish the green eyes,
the perfect features lose their flush—it was like the extin-
guishing of a rare alabaster lamp from Egypt, and curiously
painful to watch—and then he crept from the tree. He did
not wish to return to the camp. He could not endure exchang-
ing pleasantries with the soldiers or even encountering Ahinoam; and to meet Saul would remind him of Yahweh instead
of Ashtoreth. Being a shepherd, however, he knew that the
Vale of Elah, riotous with fruits and flowers ahead of their
time, had been called the Garden of Eden. He stripped to his
loincloth and made of his tunic a basket for carob nuts, black
berries, and wild pears; he wrapped a honeycomb in the huge
trumpetlike calyxes of the mulucella flowers; he cupped water
in a scarlet buttercup; and returned three times to the tree
to carry his banquet to Jonathan.

Jonathan awoke on David's third ascent and ate as
ravenously as if he had fought a battle. In spite of so rich a
feast, following so long a fever, the wild honey forestalled a
return of his nausea. They laughed and chattered without
restraint: of little things and large things, of butterflies and
eagles. Jonathan described his childhood on Crete, the war
with the Cyclopes, the storm, and the swim to Philistia.

"I'm not surprised," said David. "Everybody knows you
came from Caphtor. I just didn't know when or how."

"And you don't mind my wings?"

"Why should I? They're as perfectly formed as a snow-
flake."

"But they don't do anything."

"Neither does a luna moth, but we wouldn't want to do
without him, would we?"

"Did you really kill a lion with your bare hands, David?"

"Yes, but he wasn't very big and he had a stomach ache."

"How did you escape betrothal when you lay with a virgin at the age of twelve?"

"I told her a lion would get her if she told on me."

Then it was David's turn. "Where did you find your bear, Mylas?"

"The Philistines had trapped him on Crete and brought him to Gaza to show in a spectacle. My mother saw him in the eye of her mind and called him to me across the desert."

"Did crossing the desert turn him white?"

"All of his race are white. I expect the sun bleached them a long time ago."

"How old is your mother?"

"You might as well ask Samuel his age."

"Are you ashamed any more?"

"Of what?" asked Jonathan, surprised.

"Loving me."

"The sin of Sodom, you mean? No, I rather imagine the earthquake came on its own, not from Yahweh. It seems to me that prophets like Samuel get between us and the gods and warp our glimpse of the celestial faces. Even if Yahweh *is* angry, the worst he can do is change us into pillars of salt. Another thing. Samuel says that the Philistines are wicked idolaters. But in many ways they're just like us. They'd rather be home by the sea than racing up and down the desert. Before I got sick, I used to talk to an archer across the stream, and he said they disliked Goliath as much as we did. He ate up their best food and he had an odor and they were always having to supply him with women, some of whom he used up in a single night."

"You've changed your mind about a lot of things."

"You've corrupted me." Jonathan smiled.

"You've known me for less than a month!"

"Time is what happens to you. I would count you about ten years."

"You look like a Philistine tree god," David said, brushing a leaf from Jonathan's hair.

"It's better than looking like Yahweh, whatever *he* looks like. We aren't supposed to make images of him, but I always picture him like Samuel, all beard and bones and chattering tongue." He loosed the belt from his tunic, a band of leather inlaid with chips of turquoise. "Now I have a gift for you."

"It's a lovely gift," said David. "But you've given me a tunic already, and what can I give you in return?"

"You Israelites." Jonathan smiled. "You always think that one thing has to be paid for with another. An eye for an eye, a gift for a gift. But if you must give me something, let it be this: Let me always be first with you as long as we live."

David laughed and hugged him against his breast. "I'll promise more than that. Not even Sheol can separate us."

"Whisper," said Jonathan. "The wrong god may hear you."

Chapter

EIGHT

David, the slayer of Goliath, worked endlessly to increase his skill as a warrior. Jonathan taught him to use a spear and a sword; to feint, to wound, to kill. David, in turn, instructed Jonathan in the use of Assyrian slings. Hardened veterans, watching the Twin Archangels, as the youths had come to be called, unabashedly gathered stones in the streams and practiced against the fennecs and foxes of the desert, and no one thought to tease them for using "the toys of children."

The armies of Philistia, disheartened but not destroyed, retired to their walled cities beside the Great Green Sea, Gaza, Askelon, and Ashedod, rather like a giant squid with injured tentacles withdrawing into a cave to recover its strength and tenacity. The might of Saul's army—that is to say of Abner, Jonathan, David, and their rudely attired, ruggedly battling warriors—discouraged Israel's neighbors from open war, and the young Israelite virgins, when they went to the wells to fill their pitchers, sang of their new hero:

"Saul has slain his thousands, David his ten thousands."

If these exaggerated and heretical words came to the ears of the king, he did not acknowledge them, though David sensed an increasing suspicion in the king's behavior toward him. When David had first appeared in the camp at Michmash, Saul had politely requested him to sing and play his lyre, praised his performance, and ordered a scribe to record the words on stone tablets or papyrus scrolls. Now, even if he closeted David from his men and, incidentally, the young virgins, he ordered him to play until David's arms felt as heavy as copper and his mind was emptied of songs. Some of the time Saul was mired in madness or wearily climbing back to sanity, with little interest in ruling a kingdom which badly needed a ruler, or building an army which badly needed a commander to assist the aging Abner and the youthful Jonathan. He sighed and slept when Samuel denounced him and announced that Yahweh had withdrawn his favor, or when the people whispered that it was David, the slayer of Goliath, who would receive the anointing balm of royalty.

"Find that shepherd boy," Saul would shout, whether at cockcrow time or lamplighting time, and then, with David kneeling before him, he would raise his hand to hush the chatter of Rizpah and Michal and order David to sing. It was a familiar sight to see Saul hunched on his throne of Lebanese cedar, in the thick-walled, turreted stronghold which served as both fort and palace at Gibeah, listening to psalms of thanksgiving or paeans of victory.

"Do you think," asked David of Jonathan, going to meet their men, "that anyone suspects how it is with us?"

Jonathan smiled a slow, mischievous smile. "Who would dare to accuse the son of the king and the killer of Goliath?" Having faultlessly behaved for twenty years, he reveled in a sin for which at worst he might be stoned to death; at best, be exiled to the Desert of Sin. "We're comrades in battle. We're devoted friends. That's the way we look to the people. My mother knows, of course, but not Rizpah, nor even Michal. Saul? He hardly seems to know we're friends. To him, you're still the lute player from Bethlehem. Why, he's forgotten it was you who killed Goliath. In his ravings, he's the hero of Elah."

Jonathan . . . David loved to speak the name. It was charged both with wonder and familiarity, as wonderful as a phoenix, as familiar as a loaf of wheaten bread. Jonathan was no longer the stoically smiling, forever dutiful prince whom David had met at Michmash. His smile was not a conceal-ment, it was a revelation, and laughter welled from his lips like water from the stone struck by Moses' rod. Except for his skill in battle, he seemed younger than his years, but not in the sense that he had made of his tent a child's playroom and retreated into its solitude as if he could arrest time. It was no longer as if he were escaping into the past, but bringing the past into the present; or rather, seeing the present with the wondering eyes of a child. He was young in enjoyment of the moment and expectation of the future. The alabaster statue was flushed with roseate flickerings of life. Saul and most of Israel, if they knew the truth, would say that it had cracked and stained. To David, it was infinitely more desirable for its humanizing imperfection.

Ahinoam too had enjoyed a change. She has forgotten the insult of her rejection, the people said, the women at their looms, the farmers tilling their fields with the plowshares which had been their weapons. Poised in midsummer, she has returned to spring, and where does she learn the happy airs she sings, those sweet, tinkling lines which end like bell notes, so different from the loose, free-swinging psalms of Israel? When she sang her "Hymn to Ashtoreth," no one except for Samuel and the priests of Yahweh raised a protest:

> I am the leaves green-tender on the vine,
> The grapelets swelling into purple bait
> To tempt the bee, that harvester of air.
> I am the honied freight
> Cradled in baskets by sun-coppered hands;
> The wine press cornucopia-heaped with fruit,
> The dancing feet that liberate the juice,
> The piper with his flute. . . .

"We'll return to Elah and swim in the stream," said David.

"And Mama will pack us a lunch of quinces and turtle-dove eggs."

"And we'll sleep in your tree house."

"With only the stars for company. The Giant Bear will watch over us and guard against ghouls and Liliths."

They visited Elah, and Endor too, a town where witches pretended to be wives and plied the twin trades of sorcery and prostitution, and David's family in Bethlehem, and the sacred stones of Gilgal, planted by Joshua, and David thought: The country is almost unified for the first time since the death of Joshua. A few more wars, a few more years, and Jonathan will sit on the throne, and I will lead his armies, and the ports of Phoenicia and Philistia will hold our round-bellied merchant ships and the pharaoh of Egypt will send us gaming boards of agate and onyx, and papyrus scrolls with the Book of the Dead inscribed in hieroglyphics which look like scarabs or lightning flashes.

David, now eighteen, had never remained in love for more than a month, nor met a girl whose company pleased him as much as her body. The pleasures of Jonathan, however, seemed to him both various and invariable. David loved him for his sculptured features, bronzed with the sun, and his unimaginably yellow hair, yellower than the bands on a bumblebee, and his eyes, which seemed to have borrowed their green from the seas at the edge of the world. He loved him too for the gentle but powerful sensuality which he had aroused in a youth accustomed to an unnatural asceticism.

But Jonathan's beauty was not his chief attraction. He surprised and captivated David with a manner which was at once humility and awe. He treated a sphinx-moth, a goldfinch, a fox as if they were creatures of wonder, and even inanimate objects like stones or streams aroused him to praise. For example, he built a garden behind the palace in Gibeah, with little paths wandering among stone animals—bears, cheetahs, hyenas, fennecs, foxes—and clumps of oleander bushes and tamarisks tended as carefully as children, watered, trimmed and shaded from the withering sun.

"It's for the Great Mother because she helped you against Goliath," Jonathan explained. Israelites did not as a rule grow gardens for the sake of beauty. They had fought the barren land to eke a thin subsistence or fought ungenerous neighbors for a richer land, and to them a garden was meant to supply food. A tree should give fruit or shade. A stream should turn mill wheels or fill pitchers. It was the same practicality which had inspired the law against the Sin of Sodom. The Israelite elders, Jonathan explained, argued that a man's love for a man was an affront to nature; a barrenness which would first limit the birth of children, then the number of soldiers, then Israel's power to defend herself against her enemies. Like a garden of chrysanthemums, it produced no practical benefits; the elders therefore decreed that men should love only women and father many children.

"But Ashtoreth knows there will always be men to love women. If men love men, why not let them honor the Goddess in another way? Let them affirm the order and beauty of her creation by a continual hymn of praise—your psalms, my garden, and most important, our love. To love means to link; to link means to express the continuity of life, the unity of existence."

"Jonathan, you sound like a Philistine philosopher."

Jonathan laughed. "Truly, David? It's the Lady who speaks through me, but she has had her say. Let's continue our worship. You sing a song to her while I work in her garden."

And David sang:

> "Listen! Ashtoreth is in the corn.
> The lithe stalks bend beneath her subtle hands
> And sigh to fill the furrows of her path.
> Now still she stands,
> Inviolate as stone. . . ."

At first the garden looked strange and useless to him. A path ought to lead to a house or a road and not meander like an undecided snake. And rocks—who ever heard of piling them into animals—hyenas at that, which everybody except Jonathan disliked—and crouching them not among edible vegetables but inedible narcissi? (*"Thou shalt make no graven image. . . ."*)

"We could at least grow some carrots," said David. "A garden ought to be good for *something*."

"But that's the point." Jonathan smiled. "It has no practical purpose. It simply is."

David shook his head. "I feel as if I ought to be practicing with my bow."

"Practicing, practical. We hear too much of those words. Here, hand me that stone."

David obeyed with a wistful smile. "Do you know," he said, "that you are as stubborn as I am? I'm going to call you the lovable tyrant. What's more, in a strange kind of way, we have changed places with each other."

"No," said Jonathan. "Our souls have knit, that's all."

Soon David was helping to build an elephant, a beast which neither he nor Jonathan had ever seen but which they had heard described by an Egyptian traveler who had seen the descendants of the elephants imported from Nubia by the boy-pharaoh Pepi.

"The snout's too long," said David with finality.

"It's supposed to be long enough for him to dash water over his back."

"This way he will trip over it or snare it in thickets. And whoever heard of such ears? They look like oversized parasols. Does he raise them over his head to keep out the sun?"

"Everything ought to be big except his eyes. The ears are for swatting flies."

"He's as uncouth as a camel," muttered David, who, like most Israelites, ranked camels and dogs—the first intractable, the second verminous—among the lowest animals and infinitely below asses and oxen.

"Not uncouth, just different," said Jonathan. "Am I uncouth because of my wings?"

The finished elephant sported a long snout and preternaturally large ears.

Sometimes Michal helped them in the garden. A woman's tasks—weaving, drying flax on the flat-roofed palace—did not interest her. She respected their frequent need for solitude and sensed, too, when they would like her company. She offered good advice about the garden, whose purpose—or purposelessness—she understood more quickly than David. She discussed the rumor that the Philistines were building bronze chariots in their foundries near Gaza. She openly admired David's ruddy looks, and yet looked up to Jonathan as the ideal against whom she must measure even David. All in all she was frequently welcome, and David admired her trim runner's body, resembling that of her brother, and the sun-bronzed skin, almost honey-colored, which would have made carmine or kohl an affront to her face. David suspected that he would have fallen in love with her had it not been for Jonathan. Though her beauty to that of Jonathan and Ahinoam was the Nile compared to the Great Green Sea, and though she lacked their command of magic and the magic of their persons, she was frank, open, and highly companionable, and she made no secret of loving David, whom she called the Red Warrior because of his hair.

One afternoon, when the sun was a pleasant prickle instead of a blaze, they showed her the stone elephant.

"His snout is too long," she pronounced.

Before Jonathan could defend his creation, a shadow fell across their path. Saul had approached on soundless sandals and paused, unspeaking, to watch the work in the garden. David smiled at him and tried to assess his mood. For the moment, he seemed both sane and amiable, the father and not the madman. It was his curse that a simple farmer had multiplied into many selves, and he could not make them work in unison; he was now one person, now another, and the two, the three, the four were distinct personalities, and one of them at least was distinctly dangerous. David likened him to a cart drawn by wild asses, each pulling in a different direction notwithstanding the frantic instructions of the driver.

"It's good to see my children at play," he beamed. "We've had enough of war." In the bright afternoon light, he looked bent and gray—if not old in years like Samuel, he was old in burdens—but he had gained weight at Gibeah and people whispered that he was a better king when he delivered judgments for his subjects, sentencing thieves, condemning usurers, than when he had sat for a month with his army at Elah facing Goliath and the Philistines across the stream.

He opened his arms to Michal and kissed her undisciplined hair.

"Michal, my heart, I have always said that you could choose your own husband. Am I right in thinking that you have made your choice?"

Michal blushed and began to stammer. "Father, I have made no choice. I liked Agag, but Samuel slew him."

He turned to David. "And what have you to say, my boy?"

David did not need to deliberate his answer. Michal loved him, of that he was sure, and she would, he hoped, become a biddable bride who, underestimating its power and overlooking its passion, would not object to his friendship with Jonathan. Furthermore, it was good to be captain over a thousand men in time of war, but now, in peace, he had no official duties except as lutist to the king.

"I have long aspired to your radiant daughter's hand," said David, who knew that Saul, having once been an unlettered farmer, delighted in courtly speeches. "But who am I, a simple shepherd from Benjamin, to join the noble House of Kish?"

"Say no more. Your great-grandfather Boaz was a man of means and generosity. Though he married the foreign Ruth, he quickly won her to Yahweh. You yourself have proven to be a splendid warrior and a loyal subject. Does the choice please you, Michal?"

"Oh, yes, yes, may Ashtoreth be blessed!"

Saul shook his head with mock severity. "It was not Ashtoreth who delivered us from the Philistines."

"But it is she who understands a maiden's heart." Everyone knew that Michal's room held a shrine of Ashtoreth or images of the Goddess. Yahweh was a man's god. The women of Israel, though they followed his commandments and observed his festivals, sometimes gave their hearts to the Goddess, who was courtesan, wife, and mother.

"Perhaps you are right. At any rate we shall celebrate your betrothal as soon as you like."

"Soon?" asked Michal to David, no longer the boyish companion to her brother and his friend, but a soft young virgin enraptured with her first love.

"Soon." David smiled. "Jonathan, aren't you going to congratulate us?"

"May Yahweh look kindly on your union and bring you many sons," said Jonathan, turning his back to smooth a stone in the elephant's side.

"Come now, my daughter, leave our young men to their elephantine labors and walk to the palace with me. We must tell Rizpah our news. Ahinoam too. She will know how to manage a betrothal feast in the grand manner. In my own youth, we shared a fatted calf, exchanged vows, and that was that. But now I suppose there must be bridal gowns and processions by torchlight and—well, we shall leave the arrangements to Ahinoam, who has a gift for such niceties."

David and Jonathan remained with the elephant, David bemused by his sudden rise in fortune. To become the husband of the king's favorite daughter! To become Jonathan's brother-in-law!

Jonathan kicked the leg of his elephant and the whole outlandish beast, oversized ears, longish snout, and diminutive eyes, crumbled to their feet in a cloud of dust.

"Jonathan, what's the matter?"

Jonathan's eyes were full of tears. "I hate peace," he said. "People get married in peaceful times and bear children. In war we could be together always."

"It's war you hate, not peace. You've always said so. And

you knew I would marry one day. You even suggested Michal, because you love both of us."

"Better Michal than Merab," he sighed. "I didn't think you would marry her so soon, though. I was vain, wasn't I? To think I could keep you making gardens or throwing spears with me when you might be lying with Michal and producing the next heir to the throne."

Ashtoreth had gone out of David's day. Till now, the prospect of marriage had not meant a broken bond between him and Jonathan, but a bond which made him irrevocably Jonathan's brother. His flexible conscience allowed him to marry a girl and remain her brother's lover. A man's duty to a woman, he reasoned, was to father her children and provide for their safety and security. He was obliged to esteem her but not to love her.

"Jonathan," he cried. "Michal is a waterhole in the desert, but you are the Promised Land! Could she ever come before you?"

"Of course you must marry," Jonathan sighed. "And Michal will make you a faithful and loving wife. And I'll be your friend forever, even if I have to make elephants by myself."

"But you'll marry too, Jonathan, one of these days, and your son will be heir to the throne, not mine."

Jonathan shook his head. "I suppose I could marry. I like women. I like to talk to them. Their small talk puts me at ease, and I don't have to think about things like battles and sieges and armor. As for Michal and my mother, I love both of them very much, and I even love Merab when she's scolding me. And I would rather worship Ashtoreth than Yahweh. But I just don't think I want to marry. You can't be quiet with a woman. They expect sweet talk most of the time. If they wear a new robe and you forget to mention it, you get a cold supper without wine. And they're always after you to have babies, and more babies, and they *never* leave you alone with your friends. The only exceptions I know are my mother and, I hope, Michal."

"You might experiment before you decide against marriage," David suggested. "Not a virgin, Yahweh forbid, because then you would have to marry her. I was thinking of a harlot, though Saul has driven them out of Gibeah."

"Except Rizpah," Jonathan reminded him.

"She's retired. She doesn't count. All the others are gone. But they still flourish in towns like Endor, and the nice thing about them is that they *help*. They don't just lie there and wait as if they were expecting the Red Sea to open. And when you want to be alone, you pay your shekels and dismiss them with a compliment."

"I'll think about it," said Jonathan. Resolutely he knelt to rebuild his elephant. But his shoulders were hunched and he looked like a sad little boy whose toys had been nibbled by mice.

David embraced him and took the pale and forlorn face between his hands, and, because there appeared to be no one closer than the palace, which was hidden by poplar trees, kissed him on the mouth.

He did not hear Rizpah's approach, he felt her shadow shut them from the sun. (Two visitors, two shadows. What was the proverb brought out of Egypt? "One shadow cools, two shadows kill.") He looked into her wide, bland eyes and wondered if they concealed a perception which only Saul had perceived.

He released Jonathan as casually as if he had been adjusting his friend's tunic and said quickly, "I'm going to marry Michal. Has Saul told you?" He was careful to make his voice sound happy and expectant like that of a new bridegroom.

"Yes. I came to congratulate you. I feel that you are well suited to each other." She was wearing her usual soiled robe, originally red but discolored with saffron flour from the palace kitchen, which fell to her supervision. She might have been an aging slave instead of a concubine who had replaced a queen.

"Jonathan was wishing me success in my marriage." Even in undemonstrative Israel, fathers kissed their sons and brothers kissed their brothers, but not on the mouth, no, never on the mouth. Perhaps, however, customs differed among Rizpah's people, the Ammonites, and she would interpret the kiss as merely fraternal.

"Jonathan has become a very affectionate boy since you came to court." Irony? Reproach? Threat? Spoken by Saul, the words would have bristled with sinister implications. But Rizpah's simplicity was the perfect disguise.

"I too wish you success," she said, "though love is not

always successful, is it? There are too many ghosts." She smiled wanly and disappeared down the trail.

"Is she going to tell the king?" David asked.

"It's hard to say," said Jonathan. "She likes you, I know, and she loves Michal. But I've always taken my mother's part against her, and I rather think she dislikes me. She may go directly to Saul. Or to Michal. Or she may do nothing at all. She isn't the fool she seems, you know. She doesn't think, but she does feel, and some of her intuitions are worthy of a Siren. Have you ever noticed how often she begins a sentence with 'I feel'?"

"Never mind," said David. "Saul won't have us stoned for kissing each other."

"Probably not," said Jonathan. "But he may separate us. I can see him sending you to fight the Philistines and me to fight the Edomites. I'd rather be stoned!"

"Jonathan, nobody can separate us, not even the king." Marriages of state, unpredictable concubines, compromising kisses, even another war . . . such circumstances were like locusts, pestiferous but not dangerous (yet a plague of locusts had brought famine to Egypt).

"David, you make good things happen because you want them to, and you work like Jacob for anything you want. But there are some things that even you can't accomplish. It was too perfect, our loving each other. You know what they say: 'Perfection belongs to the gods. Show them your imperfections and then they will answer your prayers.'"

"I've shown them enough imperfections for both of us," laughed David.

"I think," said Jonathan slowly, "that you will be king one day. And Michal will be your queen."

It was the next day in the garden that an old man, as full of years as Abraham before his death, beckoned to David with yellow, crooked fingers. Unlike Abraham, who had worn his age like a mantle of white egret feathers, he resembled a fallen eagle. His talons were broken but his eyes were keen and fierce.

His voice was surprisingly soft when he said:

"My son, you are Yahweh's chosen to rule his people."

Chapter
NINE

It was a hardship; indeed, it was a deprivation to be a Siren and not to live by the sea; to live in a streamless village whose single well erupted from sulfurous Sheol. It had been worse than a deprivation to leave the coves of Crete with their sea caves and rainbow fish, the sun-drenched forests where woodpeckers chattered to Dryads, and come to the squalid town of Endor, which lay directly between Philistia and Israel and changed masters as often as the moon changed phases. But here she was safe from the pirates who scourged the coast; here she was comfortable, even if not wealthy, from her alternating practice of prostitution and soothsaying. When the Philistines controlled the town, she practiced either art; when the hardbitten, guilt-ridden Israelites ousted the permissive Philistines, she concealed her powdered newt and eye of toad in her cellar and gave herself totally, if discreetly, to love.

Often she wondered about that other Siren who had come from Crete to Israel, her friend Ahinoam. Alecto pitied her, since the king she had married was frequently mad and, even when sane, preferred the frumpish concubine Rizpah, and Ahinoam must endure the agonies of the chaste or risk being stoned by envious wives. At least the Goddess had befriended both of them by disposing of their mutual enemy, the Cyclops Goliath.

She was filling a pitcher at the well when she saw the strangers. Since the good wives of Endor avoided her company, she was careful to visit the well in the late afternoon, when no one dipped water except the thirsty travelers who paused to break their journey and seek a lodging for the night, and the dying sun laid a many-colored mantle over the

108

colorless town. The bucket tinkled melodiously as it rose on its chain with its precious freight. Quietly she hummed the ancient song with which her unprincipled ancestors had tried to ensnare Odysseus, and a voice in her whispered: "Something remarkable is going to happen to me tonight."

The men had muffled their faces with their robes, but they stared at her curiously and, she was pleased to note, admiringly, although one seemed shy and looked at the well whenever she met his gaze. Their eyes bespoke youth. With a Siren's keen vision she could even detect their color in the diminishing light of dusk. The shorter, stockier youth had eyes of penetrating blue; his friend had eyes of green which made her think of lost islands and limitless oceans (*I have known such eyes . . .*).

"The water is a trifle brackish, I fear." She smiled. "But this is Endor, forgotten and decaying, like a backwater of the sea."

Blue Eyes was quick to answer. "But not its women. Is this Rebecca I see before me, as Jacob saw her at the well?"

"Please," whispered Green Eyes to his friend. "She doesn't look like a whore. She may be somebody's wife. You'll have her husband on our necks."

"She's a whore," said Blue Eyes. "Can't you tell by her boldness? And she comes alone to a well at dusk and *without a veil.*"

Of course she had heard them; not even a whisper escaped a Siren's ears. "It pleases you to call me a whore," she said without anger. "And you are right. Long ago I learned that I have one gift. I am neither quick nor clever. I can weave a basket of rushes and grow a passable garden, but I keep house more to the satisfaction of mice than men. All in all, I would make a barely tolerable wife and a forgetful mother. But Ashtoreth has seen fit to give me an ample body and, I hope, a not unpleasing face. Since they are my best possessions, I use them to best advantage. If I were proud, I might call myself by the high-sounding name of courtesan and make you think that I had lain with kings, or better yet, I could pretend to be a widow who was waiting to marry the brother of her deceased husband. But pride goeth before a fall, and I have fallen far too many times already to risk another bruise. I am, as you say, a whore. The question that remains is this. Do I please you—either or both—and have you the wherewithal to engage my lodging and my person for the night? That is to say, if either of you pleases *me*. I have yet to decide."

Blue Eyes opened a pouch at his belt and withdrew a handful of the flat copper shekels.

"I have decided," she said.

"My friend wishes to engage you for the night," said Blue Eyes.

"Can't he speak for himself?"

"I wish to engage you for the night," said Green Eyes, though she quickly surmised that he would prefer his friend. It was not that he was foppish or fey. His voice was deep and manly in spite of his shyness, his figure straight as the mast on a galley. He was probably a stalwart warrior. Nor was he brash and assertively male, the lover who tries to conceal his inclinations with boasts and extravagant compliments. It was the way he looked at her which revealed his secret: as if she were his sister. She felt that he liked her but loved his friend; certainly he loved his friend. They stood so inseparably close that their arms must be touching beneath their robes.

Well, no matter. She was used to pleasing men, from virgins to masochists. Fathers had brought her their sons and asked her to teach them the art of love, and old graybeards had visited her for reassurance that they could still serve Ashtoreth as well as Yahweh. It was a point of pride that she could satisfy any man of any race, even if he was impotent or a lover of other men. After all, she was a Siren, and Sirens—their persons as well as their possessions and their arts—were the ultimate aphrodisiacs.

To Blue Eyes she said, "There's an inn down the road. It'll do for the night, if you don't mind fleas and thieves. That is, unless you want to come with us and watch."

Blue Eyes laughed and a red tendril of hair escaped from his hood. "I'm a doer, not a watcher." Then to his friend, "I'll see you in the morning. If the evening doesn't go well, come any time you like."

The two engaged in whispered conversation.

"But what do I *do*? I mean, to get started. She'll expect compliments and gewgaws and who knows what amorous tricks."

"Ask her price. Give her the shekels in advance and make

clear they're all you have, so you won't be robbed in your sleep."

"Then—?"

"Compliment her. Treat her like a bride. Don't make her feel you're buying her but wooing her."

"I get tonguetied when I have to compliment a strange woman. I haven't your eloquence. I'll either wind up on the street or betrothed."

"You can be as eloquent as Samuel when you want to. Now get on with it before you change your mind."

"Alecto's hut had earned her the local
name 'the Witch of Endor.'"

She looked intently into Green Eyes' face and took his hand. "You will do nicely, my dear," she said and led him, shivering, into what, on the outside, was indistinguishable from the other rounded huts of wattle and brick, which resembled a crooked row of horseshoe crabs. The inside of Alecto's hut, however, had earned her the local name "the Witch of Endor."

The boy gasped. "It's like a seacave." A fisherman's net hung like a tapestry on the far wall, and she had strung it with murexes, conch shells, and starfish. The masthead of a Philistine galley, a great wooden goose, presided over the room like a guardian god, but the true god was the Goddess, whose image in terra-cotta, life-sized, stood beside the goose as if to say: "I am the one who really sails the ships—or sinks them." She was exquisitely carved and expertly painted with red ocher and powdered lapis lazuli, and Alecto was very proud that a priest who was also a sculptor, Philistine needless to say, since there were no Israelite sculptors, had called her image "lovelier than any in Gaza or Gath, and almost as lovely as *you*." She had not charged him a shekel for the night.

The other walls hung with the shields which Philistine sailors fastened to the hulls of their ships, the shields which, staring like dragon eyes, had struck demonic terror into the hearts of the Egyptians when the Philistine war galleys had first invaded their waters. The couch rested on a framework of oars carved with tiny figures of sailors and fishermen. The pillows danced with embroidered tarpons. The drinking cups leaped with flying fish. A fresh salty scent pervaded the room, and Alecto noticed with pleasure that a look of wonderment had come into the boy's eyes, as if he were remembering sea-girt islands and malachite seas.

The better to admire the room, he thrust the robe away from his face and revealed a luxuriance of hair so yellow that it seemed to have been woven on looms within the sun. How could she fail to recognize the prince of Israel? His beauty and bravery were as famous as his friendship with David, who, she realized, had been his blue-eyed friend.

She could not restrain the cry, "Bumblebee!"

He looked at her in astonishment. "You know me?"

"Yes, my dear. I knew you as a little child. And I know why you must come to me, a whore, though the women of

Israel clamor for your attention. Has your mother told you about our race, the Sirens?"

"A little."

"Then she has told you that there is only one mature female, the queen, and many drones—the workers don't count —in each of our hives, and the males must console each other, except in the nuptial flight."

"The Tragic Exaltation, Mama called it. But it holds no attraction for me. And that's why I still cleave to men instead of women."

"And the present man being David, I may not be able to help you. He looks like a harvest god. That glory of flaming hair! It positively aureoles him."

He smiled with pleasure at her praise of his friend, and she warmed with the sweetness of him.

"I'm glad I found you. Mama would have sought you a long time ago except for my father—that is, stepfather. She was afraid she would endanger you—reveal you as a sorceress, a Cretan, a Siren. He never lets her talk about her old life. She didn't even tell me about my past until a few weeks ago, when I met David and—"

"Loved him? And thought you had committed a terrible sin, the Sin of Sodom?"

"Yes. Before I had even touched him, I felt like a leper. But now we are lovers."

"Then why do you need me?"

"David is going to marry my sister." He might have said: "David is going to die."

"And you are hurt and angry and want to show him you can possess a woman too?"

"No," he said. "I've come for practice. One day I will probably have to marry too—to produce an heir, don't you see. And I have to know what to do. My bride will undoubtedly be a virgin, and if I'm as ignorant as she is, we'll probably spend our wedding night playing draughts. I've never been with a woman. I think you are very beautiful, but even so I don't want to—I don't know how to—"

"Lie with me, Jonathan? The first thing is to feel that you don't have to. If we spend the whole night in conversation, why, nothing is lost, and no one will ever know that you were not the most exhilarating lover of my life. First, though,

I shall cook you a supper. Love languishes on an empty stomach."

In spite of her disavowal of domesticity, she prepared a succulent dinner of quail cooked in figs, wheaten bread in which raisins swam like minnows, and a pudding whose ingredients she carefully withheld from him because they included a generous amount of powdered mandrake roots, the strongest aphrodisiac in Israel. "Now for some beer," she said. "I expect you don't often get that, do you?"

"Ususally I drink milk or wine." Beer, an import from Philistia, was looked upon with suspicion by the elders of Israel. "However—"

"There now, you've had enough."

Jonathan, finishing the beer in his cup with one big gulp, blurted. "About this lovemaking. Won't you, uh, disembowel me? After all, I'm a drone."

Alecto said with professional pride. "You forget that I am a courtesan as well as a Siren. The usual queen—your mother, for example, if she still ruled a hive—disembowels her lovers by the frenzy of her passion. After all, she must wait a year for that one little moment of satisfaction and make do with an inexperienced drone who probably has a friend. Furthermore, she feels that she is honoring him by sending him directly to the Celestial Vineyard."

"It's an honor I can do without."

"Exactly. You don't want to go without David. Besides, in Israel, who knows if you would wind up in the Vineyard or in Sheol? My point is that I will pleasure you so soothingly that you needn't fear the loss of any vital organs, genitals, abdomen, what have you. I am a Siren. I am also a courtesan who has raised lust to art, and love to genius. Forgive my boasting. I only want you to trust me."

"May I have another cup of beer?"

"Certainly not."

"But I'm feeling so relaxed. So warm and light. As if I could float through the ceiling."

"That's the danger. To quote a Siren philosopher who has often been plagiarized, 'Too much drink excites desire but limits performance.'"

"Oh," he said with disappointment. "Some more raisin cake then."

"Why don't you remove your robe? You look as if you

were dressed against a winter night in the hinterlands of Assyria. Allow me to be your blanket."

He visibly winced at the offer.

"Jonathan, my sweet, is my body so repellent to you?"

"Oh, no," he cried. "You're a real Eve! It was what you said about being a blanket."

"David said the same thing?"

"Yes," he sighed.

"And said it better. Then I shall be a light linen coverlet. Different, you see. Not his competitor but his ally." She left the room and returned in a gossamer robe beneath which the splendors of her body showed with misty allurement, the painted nipples, the navel inset with a malachite, the long, powerful, yet feminine legs which had once propelled her through the sea with the speed of a flying fish. Total nudity could only alarm Jonathan; an intimation, she hoped, would excite him.

He sat uneasily in his loincloth beside a brazier. The firelight flickered over his honey-colored skin. How young and unblemished he looked to her! Did he understand, had his mother told him, that the life of a Siren, a drone no less than a queen, might outlast a civilization? That splendid David might wrinkle into winter while Jonathan walked in the summer of youth? And yet there was something about him which suggested a short life, a look not so much of fragility as of mortality. Perhaps, after all, mortal David would outlive him to rule a kingdom.

Enough of her morbid thoughts, enough of his apprehensive looks. She must break the mood.

"You look like a frightened fennec," she teased. "Your ears are quivering under that mass of golden hair."

"One of those little foxlike creatures with the solemn faces and the big ears." He smiled. "Yes, I expect I do. It's so complicated, you see, this getting seduced. I must be a very difficult customer. Most men would have dragged you onto your couch and taken their pleasure at once."

"Your heritage is against you," she reminded him. "Too many drones, too few queens. For a thousand years the drones have made do with each other."

"David had trouble with me too at first. I got sick. But later it was like entering the Celestial Vineyard."

"You've been brought up on Israelite notions of sin.

They're hard to forget. Every time the good wives of the town glare at me, I know I am thought a sinner. Yet they come to me for potions and philters and ask my advice about love. Are you feeling sick now?"

"No, David got me over that. It's rather humorous when you stop to think about it—what men and women do together for pleasure. When I was a boy I watched a friend of my sister's coupling with one of Saul's soldiers. All those wiggling parts, the sighs, and the squeals! They were inexperienced and didn't seem to know what went where. For both of them, it must have been like putting on a suit of armor for the first time. The Goddess, I think, has a sense of humor."

"There ought to be laughter in love," she agreed. "But there ought also to be wonder. How ever often I've lain with a man—and I choose my men, even as they choose me—I've never failed to give and to gain pleasure, and that, in this dusty, Goddess-forsaken country is something for which to be thankful."

"I can't get the two together. The wonder and the laughter. Except with David. With him, it's hardly physical at all. I don't even tell my body what to do. I transcend myself."

"Have I plied you with sufficient beer to make you feel a trifle transcendent?"

"I might have one more cup."

"Something to lessen the ordeal, eh?" She began to exhale a subtle musk from her lungs.

His eyes grew kind and grave. "You think I don't appreciate your beauty or that I find you too old for me. Neither is true. I never thought another woman could approach my mother in beauty, but you could pass for her sister, if your hair were blond. But the trouble is, I want to put you in a temple instead of onto a couch. As for age—well, I just don't think about that. You may be two hundred—"

"One hundred and sixty," she said with affronted dignity.

"—for all I care. The point is, you look about twenty-five. No, age isn't the trouble. It's the other. You remind me of my mother and the Goddess."

"Come and lay your head in my lap and I will sing you a song."

Jonathan dutifully obeyed and, scenting the musk, remarked that she smelled like the sea. "Flying foam and salty winds—like your house, but better." She bent and kissed him on the cheek. He looked at her with unmitigated trust, confident that she would somehow sail him to the Scylla-guarded islands of love.

She began to sing. Perhaps the song was about herself and Jonathan.

THE WINDFLOWER AND THE WIND

"The windflower loves the wind
As an albatross the sea,
A marigold the morning sun,
And bergamot the bee.

The wind who spreads her bud
With a roving, boyish gust
And whispers her to sleep at night
In a bed of pollen dust.

The windflower loves the wind,
But does that wanderer care?
However he may whisper love,
His heart is made of air."

Hardly had she ended the song than one of her presentiments came to her as vividly and suddenly as a flight of Harpies. Sometimes men visited her to seek the future and she had to tell them: "I see nothing. Trust to the Goddess." At other times, the future would intrude upon the present, like a blood-red rain or a river overrunning its banks. She saw Jonathan in battle. The Israelites had been routed by Philistine chariots. Even now a Cyclops and his driver were bearing down on him in a huge chariot with armored sides and great iron wheels, which thundered and crackled over the pitted earth. The Cyclops was drawing his bow and glaring maliciously through his single eye. Was it true what they said in the market place: "Saul has forfeited Yahweh's favor. He and his sons will meet in Sheol?"

"What is it?" he asked. "There are tears in your eyes. Have I hurt your feelings?"

"Not you, my dear. A vision I had, that's all. These fancies come to me at times. Memories of the happy days on Crete."

She had found the one way to win him as a lover. She had made him pity her. He kissed her on the mouth, and then he took her with a tenderness like the descent of a god.

The next morning she returned the shekels with which he had paid for the night. "You didn't buy my love," she said. "I gave it to you."

"Perhaps," he said, "if it were not for David—"

"Ah, but there is David."

"Yes, there is." He smiled radiantly as if it were he who was contemplating a god. The loss of him was like a fisherman's hook in her heart.

"Still, for a little while, you loved me too. It wasn't that you subtracted from the love you bore David. Rather you added to it. Remember me, Jonathan."

"As long as I live," he promised and held her in a chaste goodbye.

She drew away from him before she had to say: "You may forget me very quickly then. But I will bear your son."

Chapter

TEN

Saul had settled his family in the palace at Gibeah, which, in spite of its formidable walls and turrets, remained a place in which to live from day to day as well as take refuge from invaders; to mingle in the throne room where Saul delivered judgments and righted wrongs or to seek solitude in the upper chambers with only the mice for company. The marriage of David, slayer of Goliath, to Michal, the favorite daughter of the king, delighted a country wearily accustomed to war. Ahinoam, guiding Rizpah, arranged a wedding feast to shame a pharoah and then withdrew with her attendant, Naomi, to a vineyard and cottage beyond the town, a gift from Saul, in self-imposed exile. As for Michal, her beauty had bloomed like a rose of Sharon. The lithe young warrior maid had spent the days before her marriage at her loom to weave a wedding gown and, rapt in her dream of David, had scarcely noticed how much she owed to Ahinoam's careful instruction: its veil, its trim of Egyptian antelope fur, its embroidered design of swallows encircling a field of saffron grain.

David too had reason to rejoice. Had he not, a shepherd from little Bethlehem, accomplished a miraculous friendship and a royal marriage? But there was a locust in his manna. He had wounded Jonathan. The prince's smile was frequent but forced, and his gaiety seemed to come from a skin of wine. When David and Michal walked in the garden, Jonathan fled from the palace to visit his mother. When David played his lyre before the king, Jonathan pleaded weariness and withdrew to his silent room on the second floor and communed with Mylas, the bear. Michal, though inexperienced, was a passionate and desirable bride. But David, the bridegroom, was more dutiful than desiring. To the man accustomed to gold, can silver suffice? Is water the equal of wine?

After a week of marriage, David was a thirsty man. He was also a troubled man when he surprised Jonathan leaving the palace as unobtrusively as a servant who has stolen a casket of gems.

"My mother is alone in her new house," said Jonathan with a look of heartbroken resolution. He carried a leather bag and a bowl for feeding his bear. "I'm going to visit her."

"But you visit her almost every day as it is. And Naomi sleeps there at night."

"This time I'm going to stay. Besides, Naomi is deaf."

"When will I see you?" cried David.

"I'll come back for Mylas."

"That's not what I mean."

Jonathan said without reproach, "David, you chose."

"But you knew how it would be. It's only for a little while that we can't be alone together. Hush now. Here's Michal."

She had not overheard them. "Jonathan, my dear, where are you going?"

David answered for him. "He is going to visit your mother and then go hunting for that lion the shepherds have been complaining about. It's killed a hundred sheep. Dearest one, I would like to go with him. It isn't fit than Ahinoam should be forgotten in our happiness or that Jonathan should risk his life without his brother beside him. Remember, I have much experience with lions."

Michal sighed and enfolded David in a warm embrace.

"You're right, my love. Men need other men for company at times. A man wearies if he lounges about a palace with the womenfolk. Visit my mother and then go on your hunt. Jonathan misses your company. Next to me, he loves you best."

Jonathan brightened like a child with his first goatcart and kissed his sister tenderly on the ear. "We shall bring you the skin to make a rug."

Refusing armorbearers, they began their journey on foot before sunrise and walked in the rare communion of silence.

Finally Jonathan turned to him and smiled in the old gentle way. "Be patient with me, my brother. For a little while I was first. Second is not yet enough."

"Michal is second," said David without hesitation. "How she would grieve if she knew the truth! How much I like her, how little I love her. Every morning she looks at me as if I were going to battle and might not return. Once I mistook her for you and almost called your name."

"Do you think she guesses how it is with us?"

"No," said David. "If we were Philistines, perhaps. But in Israel it is almost unthinkable that a shepherd should prefer a prince to a princess. She takes us only for friends, and so do the people."

Jonathan smiled with mischief and squeezed David's hand. "It is fun to sin with you, David. After all, I am a Cretan drone, not an Israelite. How can I love against the custom of my race?" It was his one failure in conscience.

"We love as we must," said David, pleased to have cured his friend of guilt.

They stripped to swim in a stream and lay on its banks to dry. Jonathan did not try to conceal his wings, small, golden, and perfect, like slender flames at his back. He resembled a fallen angel who did not lament the loss of the sky. Their fingers touched and passion flared between them.

"I don't want to die," David cried with a vehemence close to rage. "To to a shadow in Sheol—is it not a terrible thing?"

"All men die, people like us first of all. The little folk sometimes hide in their hovels for many years. But death seeks out the palaces and the princes with cruel thoroughness. We have to go somewhere after death. My mother speaks of the Celestial Vineyard, but I was reared as an Israelite like you, and wherever you go I want to follow—or lead."

David shuddered at the prospect of Sheol. "I expect we shall be poor company for each other. But shadows can meet even if they can't speak."

"I don't like shadows," said Jonathan. "I don't like the night. Perhaps we can somehow climb to the Vineyard."

"Your mother says it's beyond the clouds and the stars and the reach of the Sky God. Do you think your poor little wings could lift you so high? And what about me who have none at all?"

They did not hear the approach of Philistine soldiers. Abruptly a voice said, more with amusement than threat:

"David, son of Jesse, and Jonathan, son of Saul. I see that it is Ashtoreth you serve now instead of Yahweh."

The young men jumped to their feet. They were surrounded by soldiers who looked less ominous than curious. They pointed at Jonathan's wings and one of them whispered to his mate, "From Caphtor, I warrant. A Siren's son."

A man of middle years, dressed in a purple tunic and a white sash, with a large amethyst ring on his middle finger, confronted them with a smile.

"Is it my Lord Achish of Gath I address?" Jonathan asked. They had met from a distance in battle but never crossed swords.

"It is he."

Achish was seren of Gath, a man more renowned for his strategy than his sword, more at ease in a palace beside the sea than on a foreign battlefield. He looked like a bard and, in fact, was said to have written an epic about the earthquake which had sent his people on their wanderings to Crete and then to Philistia. It was impossible to guess his age. His hair was gray, but there were no lines to mar his shaved, sun-bronzed face. He smelled of myrrh; his blue tunic was unblemished and unwrinkled even on this hot and dusty day. He would have looked at home on the deck of a ship or ruling an island humped like a giant turtle and murmurous with Tritons. David liked him.

He stared at Jonathan's wings with admiration. "I had guessed that the prince of Israel belonged to the Old Ones. His mother's beauty, to say nothing of his own, is fabled even in Philistia, and my great-grandfather knew such beings —Sirens are you called?—on Caphtor. Sometimes we even glimpse them on the coast of Philistia."

"Are we your prisoners?" Jonathan asked. "If you wish to take me because I am, as you say, a Siren, I will yield to you. But I must beg you to release my friend. He need not suffer because of me."

Achish smiled. "You have heard that in Philistia we keep the Old Ones in pools or cages and show them to the multitudes. It is one of the lies told about us in Israel. No, Jonathan, you and your friend are safe from us, and for other reasons as well. Philistia is not yet ready to resume her war with Israel. We do not like to fight. We will not fight until we know that we will win, and if we could find another homeland—an island with neither earthquakes nor invaders—we would sail away from your bleak little country forever. But I have this to say to you, David and Jonathan. You serve an old, mad king who would kill the both of you—yes, you too, Jonathan—if he knew the nature of your love. In Philistia, however, the Goddess' own son is the patron of male lovers. Come then and stay with us in our land. We will give you a walled city, Ziklag, and you shall help us to fight against the roving Amalekites who harass our borders and graze their camels among our vines. In peaceful times, you may visit the sea and inspect our ships and—who can say?— voyage to foreign lands in search of apes and ivory, frankincense and nard. We do not ask that you march against your own people when Philistia and Israel resume their war. Only that you do not fight with the Israelites against the Philistines."

David studied this enemy who offered to be a friend. "You could have killed us while we talked. In spite of the reasons you give, you do not really need to offer us asylum."

Achish smiled. "If I had killed you in each other's arms, I would have angered the Goddess and her son, who have not been unkind to me in the past. When I was young—how many lifetimes ago?—I had a friend like you. He died in a skirmish with Israelites, smitten, no doubt, by your forbidding Yahweh. But I have a long memory. My heart is a temple wherein I keep his image, perfect and immortal, like green marble. Could I murder my friend for a second time? Go now. We have killed the lion which was raiding your flocks. We heard about him from a shepherd boy and about the princes who hunted him, and I came hunting you. Invent a story for your bloodthirsty Saul. The beast had sprung at

Jonathan's throat and you, David, leapt on its back and broke its neck with your bare hands. You Israelites, so direct and practical in other ways, love such stories and never question their truth. Your famous Samson was a simple-minded rustic who lay with a painted whore. But your poets have changed him into a national hero who loved a woman with the face of a goddess. I ask only that you do not tell Saul about the Philistines wandering in his borders. Have I your word?"

"You have my word," said David.

"And mine," said Jonathan.

"Come then, both of you, and let us embrace as friends. The gray hair, the red and the gold."

"The Goddess was truly with us," David said, when the last Philistine was a stir of wind and the susurration of dust.

"I wish," said Jonathan, "that we could have gone with him. We could still overtake him if we ran."

"There would come a time when we might have to fight our own people, in spite of his promises. He speaks only for Gath. There are four other serens."

"We could have seen the sea together."

But Samuel had mentioned a throne. . . .

"Perhaps when our armies drive to the sea. Now we must return to Gibeah."

Before they returned to the palace, they visited Ahinoam's cottage. She, the great queen, more beautiful than Ruth among the sheaves, was tending violets beside her door. She rose and smiled and held them in a single long embrace.

"Is it well with you, my sons?"

"We miss you, Mama. You must be lonely here."

"Saul invited me to stay in the palace. I asked for this house because of Rizpah. Sometimes I pity her. She fears that Saul will return to me and I wished to set her at ease. Yes, it is well with me, if David and Jonathan are friends."

"We are sometimes together," said Jonathan, "but in the palace—"

"Ah, my son. The nights are long for the lover without his love. But you can endure the cold chaste stars if morning brings sun and David."

"I could almost wish for war," said Jonathan, the peaceable. "Then we could share the same tent and fight as one."

"No, my dear. The Goddess designs our lives. She helps us to grow our crops, to build our houses, to make of the forest a friend. Yahweh disrupts her plans with his petty wars and his jealous concern for one small nation. Do not tempt Sheol."

Rizpah smiled like a child and patted David's cheek. Michal examined his arms for claw marks and marveled at how he had killed the lion and saved her brother.

"Samson from the wars!" she cried. "But I am a poor Delilah."

"Better Michal without any shears!"

Her scarlet robe was dyed with the dye of the insect called the kermes and she looked like a living flame. Her passion frightened him; he did not want to pretend at love.

"Play for me," Saul commanded. "One of those tinkling melodies Ahinoam sings. The ones with lines which end with—what do you call it?—rhyme." He did not speak of their absence. Had a mood possessed him and clouded his memory? He looked neither blank nor pained, but rich in years; battle-scarred, yes, but ruddier, healthier than David had ever seen him.

"He has been well since before the wedding," Rizpah whispered.

The room was a savage place, with shields on the walls, spearstands on either side of the door, Goliath's armor standing like a guardian god, the black emptiness in his helmet a single great eye. The floor was covered with reeds; one brazier fought a chilling draft. It was neither Philistine nor Egyptian, it was purely Israelite, and it signified Israel's strength as well as her weakness, a poor people without time for the graces of life but indomitable in war and, at their infrequent best, unswervable in their ambition to unify the land and worship a single god.

David received his harp from a young attendant, a boy who looked at him as worshipfully as he had once looked at Saul, and began to play, not about battles, not in praise of Yahweh, but about a road to the sea. He addressed his song to Saul, who, hopefully, would not understand the secret allusions, but Jonathan understood them and smiled, and it was to him that David truly sang.

" 'I go,' said the wind,
'To a yonder-land
Where the dragon feeds
From a Dryad's hand,
And the Centaur blows on a silver horn
To call the unicorn.'

'Wind,' I cried,
'Like a vagabond
You drift and play
In the blue beyond
And dream your tale of a silver horn
Which calls to a unicorn.'

But the wind, he laughed
In a secret way
And climbed the clouds,
And who shall say
If he hears the call of a silver horn
And the hooves of a unicorn?"

"Jonathan!"

The name crackled like the snap of a catapult. David dropped his lyre and the strings quivered with incongruous sweetness as he stared from Saul to Jonathan.

"Jonathan, son of a perverse, rebellious woman, you have chosen the son of Jesse above your own father. Get you from my court!"

Jonathan did not flinch from the accusations.

"You wrong me, Father, as you have wronged my mother in taking Rizpah to your bed. I have not betrayed you. I have only chosen a friend."

Michal knelt at her father's feet and clasped his hand. "It is a lie you have heard, my father. David and Jonathan would serve you to the death. How can you even suspect them of treason?"

He shook free of her. "And has he got you with child? Or is he concerned with the mischief of Dagon and Ashtoreth?"

Defiant David met the king's stare. "At least I have fathered no children on concubines. Of what other sins do we stand accused, Jonathan and I?" He must know the truth. He must know if Saul knew the truth.

"Of seeking my throne," Saul muttered, his voice beginning to slur. " 'Saul has slain his thousands, David his ten thousands.' Of alienating my son."

"I have always been true to my lord," he began. "I have—"

"David!"

It was Jonathan's cry which saved his life. The spear grazed his arm and shuddered against the wall. He looked with disbelief at the "old, mad king" who could move with such menacing speed.

"Come, David," said Jonathan, and hurried him from the room. Behind them, they heard the weeping of Rizpah, the pleas of Michal, the silence of the king as he tumbled into oblivion. Perhaps, awakening, he would forget his suspicions. Perhaps the madness had become the man.

No one pursued them. No one had witnessed the incident except the two women. The guards at the door of the palace had heard the outcry but, accustomed to royal moods, nodded with sympathy when Jonathan explained that his father had suffered another fit of madness and Michal and Rizpah were tending him.

At the edge of the town, Jonathan and David paused beneath a sacred terebinth tree whose branches fluttered with colored ribbands, offerings left by virgins who hoped to win handsome husbands and bear strong sons. At just such times, when the flat world seemed tilting into chaos, Jonathan's gentleness became inflexible strength. Usually it was impossible to imagine him on the battlefield. Now he might have slain Goliath.

"You must hide for the night," he said. "If my father acted through madness, he may forget and welcome you back to his court. But if he truly believes his accusations, you must leave the country. Go to Achish in Gath. He has promised you asylum."

"Come with me, my brother. You too are in danger."

"I must stay to soften my father's heart. He will not kill me no matter what he believes. Or Achish believed." (We could have followed him to the sea, thought David.) "Remember, he has no proof. I do not think that Rizpah has told him anything. Tomorrow I will go to the forest beyond Gibeah to practice with my bow. If the arrows fall to the right of my target, you will know that the king's heart is hardened against you."

"And we will meet in the forest?"

"Yes. While I send my little armorbearer to fetch the arrows, we can briefly talk."

"My brother, I would risk Sheol rather than leave you here. Without you life is an empty gourd, a well which is stopped with sand."

"But you are the heir to the throne! Samuel himself anointed you king."

"But I never told you that!"

"Half of the country, including my father, knows. You are Yahweh's chosen."

"That vengeful desert god—"

"He has much power in these parts. And if he has chosen you even against your will, he is not to be denied. Hate him if you must. Serve him for the sake of Israel. He never asked to be loved. Only to be obeyed."

They embraced with the mute urgency of those about to die. At the last, there were no more words, only an empty gourd and a well which was filled with sand.

Chapter

ELEVEN

The sunflowers stood as tall as a man, field after field of them, their faces like those of young golden gods; Jonathan's face multiplied to infinity. *When will he come? When will he come, bringing his own dear presence and Saul's forgiveness?* For three days David had lived in hiding, sheltered by night in a small summer house trellised with grapevines, amid a vineyard adjacent to the flowers. It had been a brief exile. . . . It had seemed like forty years in the Wilderness.

He heard their voices before he saw them, the low, soft accents of Jonathan, the high, piping voice of the Midianite lad, who had broken his leg on a raid and was left to die, till Jonathan found him and trained him to carry his bow.

"I will shoot the arrows at yonder knoll," said Jonathan.

"When the last arrow is fired, fetch them for me, Pepi, and return to the palace. My father has asked me to inspect his vineyards for him."

The child sighed; he wanted to stay with his master. "May I inspect them with you? My father was a vintner before he became a raider." (David, impatient, tore a vine from the wall and kneaded the green pulp in his hand.)

"Not this time, Pepi."

"I'm always being sent somewhere," the child protested. "You won't even let me fight the Philistines with you. Or chase the rene—renegade David."

"David is an exile, not a renegade. You would love him if you knew him as I do."

"I do know him, and I don't like him at all. You were always with him until he married the princess, and he never even noticed me."

"Do as I say. Now." Jonathan's authority was quiet but implacable.

Twang, twang, twang, sang the bow, like a hoarse-throated lyre, as it scattered its arrows to the right of the knoll.

"Ah, my aim is off today, Pepi."

"Perhaps my lord drank too freely at the Feast of the New Moon," Pepi teased him.

"Perhaps," said Jonathan, and David imagined the kindly smile, the pat on the boy's shoulder from one whose greatest intoxication had come from love.

Jonathan approached the summer house with careful, measured steps, lifting a vine aside from the path, pausing as if to inspect a tumbling trellis. Pepi, though out of sight, could still hear Jonathan's steps and he must not suspect his prince, who had "come to inspect a vineyard," of racing across the fields to meet a renegade. Eons seemed to pass, the world was spun out of chaos; Adam too, and Eve from Adam's rib; in the time which Jonathan took to join David.

They had been separated for a mere three days, but they looked at each other as if some change, some diminishment of love, had been wrought by the separation; and then, reassured, embraced with a wild and tender yearning.

"You have grown thinner, my brother," said David. "Do you bring ill tidings?" Sunlight above the trellis dappled

Jonathan's hair. *(Even the sun is jealous of his gold. It must summon shadows to dim the wonder.)*

"Your fears have come true," said Jonathan. "My father wishes you dead. He has told me to kill you."

"Why?" asked David. "Why, Jonathan? I would have served him until I died!"

"He is envious because the people love you and sing of your exploits when they meet at the wells. After you fled, he accused us again of plotting treason against him."

"And the other?"

"He said nothing, though I think it was in his mind. I thought at first: His threat of treason is the jealousy of a madman, and his madness will pass. But the madness has indeed become the man. He supposed us allied against him with the Philistines. Why, he even hurled his spear at me! Fortunately his aim was poor. Ahinoam spoke to him then; she had come from her house in the country when she heard of his wrath against us. She reminded him of Michmash and how I had helped him to win, and how he had summoned you to sing for him from your father's flocks. At first he called her a whore of Ashtoreth—he must have been thinking of Rizpah, who fluttered her hands in her usual helpless way. But she looked him straight in the eye and said, 'You may call me a whore all you like. Yahweh knows, I've had reason to become one since you sent me from your couch. You may hurl your spears at me and wave your hands in rage. Nevertheless, I will swear at the cost of my life to the innocence of my son Jonathan and his friend David in any plots against your throne.' Her anger quieted him. He slumped on the throne and muttered, 'Go now and leave me in peace, all of you.'

"For three days I tried to see him—in vain. I was always told by his guard, 'The king is sleeping,' or 'The king is taking his ease against the heat,' or 'The king is planning his winter campaign against the Philistines.' Today he sent this message: 'Return to my court with David's head on a stake.' "

"It is a clever and persistent demon which haunts him," said David. "Even you and Ahinoam are feeble exorcists in such a case. His madness allows him to do the things which his natural kindness forbids. He is very strong. But Samuel sapped his confidence and filled him with fear of Yahweh. Made him feel guilty when he was guiltless or show cruelty when he would have liked to be kind. And the demon flourishes. But what of Michal?"

"She is shut in her quarters. Saul refuses to see her, because she took your part. I called to her window from the ground. She said: 'Tell David to send for me in the heat of day or the dead of night. I will arise and follow him even to Sheol.'"

"If I had loved her better, perhaps it would not have gone so hard for her. At least she would have had a blither memory during my exile. I have not used her well, Jonathan."

"You were a kindly deceiver, David. She always believed that she was first with you. Would you have wanted to love her best?"

"I would change nothing. I regret nothing except that we did not meet as boys. I chose a god above a mortal, and mortals must weep. It is the condition of life." He looked into his heart and saw how little he loved the princess, how easily and guiltlessly fooled her; how many women he would love and forsake, if only because they loved him.

"Are the gods exempt from tears?"

"Divine tears are silent and dry. The cruelest tears of all."

"Perhaps you are right," said Jonathan. "When the Lady created men, it is said that she wept because there was no man without his sorrow. She stood above the world, outspreading her wings like a cloak to enfold her creation. 'My tears will fall like rain and water the parched and thirsting fields, and my people will know of my love,' she thought. But her tears were dry and she found and gave no solace. 'I will give them the gift of laughter,' she said, 'a lantern to scatter their shadows.' And only then she found peace."

"It is a lovely tale."

"It is also true, I believe."

"Such things may have happened once. But the gods must have died or forgotten. Or why do they shake the world, hurling storm against town, sea against land, Philistine against Israelite; separating lover from lover?"

"They nod, to be sure. Or wish to punish or test us. But this I know. Ashtoreth listens and sometimes she answers. Even in exile, David, speak her name and show her your heart."

"I will speak *your* name, Jonathan, for you will go with me. In Egypt, Israel is known as the Wide Wilderness, not as the Promised Land. Saul and his army will never find us among the scorpions. Remember that I was once a shepherd. I can live in a forest or on a desert. You have shown me how to strike water from rocks. My father showed me how our ancestors caught the resin of the tamarisk and called it manna. Follow me, Jonathan. Why should we part because of this vicious demon in Saul? One day you will be king, and Saul will find peace in Sheol."

"I ask only a garden in which to build elephants out of stone and a sea to sail or swim in, and David to be my friend. I will sit near your feet in the court. And we will hunt and fight together and our people will call us the Twin Archangels. But you, not I, will be king and your sons after you."

He argued vehemently against the truth. "Do you think that all this time I wanted a throne? Courted favor with Saul, married Michal?"

"It is what you want and deserve. It is what I want for you. Protect my mother and sisters and brothers and I will serve you until I die."

"And your children as well."

"I will sire no children, I think."

"Yet you lay with the Witch of Endor."

"She will not beget. There is an herb she takes."

"You have my promise. But why do you talk as if we were never to meet again? You will surely come with me into the Wilderness. Without you, I am afraid."

"Why, you never feared anything, David! At first, perhaps. But not at the confrontation. Not even Goliath once you had loaded your sling. I've watched you enough in battle. I ought to know."

"I fear loneliness. You are to blame for that."

"Wherever you go you will find new friends."

"Friendship is love without wings. I have asked you to join me. You have given no answer. I beg you to join me."

"I can't, David."

"You would have gone before, when Achish asked us," he cried. He wanted to shake him or strike him for his obstinacy. "Do you mean to return to court, where Saul has tried to kill you?"

"I have learned to anticipate his spears. There is a certain look he gets in his eye. Perhaps I can help him to fight his demon."

"He isn't even your father."

"He is the only father I know. When I was a little boy he taught me to draw a bow and duel with a sword, and I was proud to make him proud of me. I still love what the demon has not destroyed. I still love the kindness hidden deep within him, like the water at the bottom of a well, under a weight of sand. But most of all I must see to the safety of my mother and Michal. Both of them helped in your escape and earned his wrath."

David's tears were dry and mute, and yet in that secret ark of the heart which has no name, unless it is called the Holy of Holies, he was strangely glad. It seemed to him that Ashtoreth, or the Mother behind the Mother, or whatever power decreed the fates of men, had offered him one perfection, like a jacinth with a hundred glittering facets impervious to time and change. He who had been a shepherd and then a prince must now become an exile, but he would carry the jacinth with him and neither thieves nor dust could corrupt its immortal fires. But the gem would flaw and yellow unless its match was possessed by the beloved. It was said by the elders of Israel that always there is one who embraces and one who opens his arms to receive the embrace. He did not want an unequal love.

"Remember me," he said. "Remember me when you take a wife and bear children and march against the Philistines."

"Once I was a little boy who slept under a warm coverlet with his toy animals. Then I was a youth who played at war with other youths in purple helmets. I was not happy, but I knew no other life. Then I met you. I have asked myself whether it was better before you came. The long hours of dreaming in my tent. The undemanding love I bore for Nathan, my armorbearer. There was loneliness, yes, like a dagger wound that nags and will not be healed. But not like this—this wound I think is almost mortal. Still, I do not want to be healed and I do not want to sleep."

"How will it be when both of us sleep? Even Samuel, they say, descended into Sheol. Will we meet as shadows in the land of shades? Or is Sheol barred to us by Yahweh?"

"She was once our queen, your ancestress."

"In the Cretan palace where I was a little boy—so my mother says—there was a tall alabaster image of a lady with outspread wings. Sometimes the water lapped around her feet, but it never touched her gown.

" 'She was once our queen, your ancestress,' my mother said.

"Her wings fascinated me. 'What did she do with them?' I asked. (For all of our people had lost their wings, except for the little stubs you have seen on my back.)

" 'She played among the clouds.'

" 'But the Sky God is not our friend. He loves the Cyclopes.'

" 'There was a time when he loved the Goddess too.'

" 'And after the queen was tired of playing?'

" 'She flew to the Celestial Vineyard, beyond the stars.'

" 'And what is it like there, Mama?'

" 'No one has ever returned to tell us except this very queen. She loved a drone who had lost his wings in a storm and could not ascend in the nuptial flight. It was she who died before him. But some of our people saw her when she returned to lift him into the heavens.

" ' "What is death?" they cried.

" ' "A place without Cyclopes, without earthquakes, where lovers are reunited with those they love at the time they loved the most."

" 'Our people carved her statue against oblivion.' "

David sighed and clung to Jonathan's hand. "It is a lovely tale. But I am a shepherd and not a drone. Where are my wings? And your are too small for flight."

"Perhaps the Goddess will help us."

David shook his head. "I am glad that you think her capable of every miracle, and mindful of every prayer."

"I don't think, David, I hope, but what is life except a mosaic of hopes—of brightly colored stones—sard and onyx and beryl—which we polish daily and replace if they are lost? I only ask that you keep a stone in your heart. And trust me to wait for you."

"And if I die first—?"

"I shall be first—of that I am sure—for you have a kingdom to rule."

"I would like to be king," said David. "I would like to be king and unite this poor broken country. Israel is like a

lamb surrounded by wolves. She desperately needs a
shepherd."

"I understand, David. It is what you want most in all the
world."

"It is what I want next to you," said David, surprised at
the truth, for the thought of a throne was unspeakably dear
to him. He laid his hand on Jonathan's sun-warmed hair and
felt its softness like the fleece of a lamb. "You are better
than I. Gentle without being weak. But I do not think that
you would be a happy king. You have never learned how
to hate."

"I hate the evil in men, not the men themselves. But
enough of such things. David, sing me another song. This
time about yourself instead of me."

"There is an old folk song among the Israelites, a mirror
to both of us. You have heard it many times."

"Sing it again."

"O that thou wert as my brother,
That sucked the breasts of my mother!
When I should find thee without
I would kiss thee; yea, I should not be despised.
I would lead thee, and bring thee into my mother's house,
Who would instruct me:
I would cause thee to drink of spiced wine of the juice of
      my pomegranate.
Set me as a seal upon thine heart,
As a seal upon thine arm
For love is strong as death;
Jealousy is cruel as the grave:
The coals thereof are coals of fire,
Which hath a most vehement flame.
Many waters cannot quench love's fire. . . ."

"Tender comrade," said Jonathan. "For this small moment,
let us forget about thrones and exiles. We are larger than
mortal things. You are the earth and I am the sea, devoted
friends locked in eternal embrace."

"Then we must swear by blood." David withdrew the dagger from his sash, a bronze blade with an onyx hilt. He
wanted to drive it into his heart. Could Sheol be worse than
a wilderness without Jonathan?

"I will be first," said Jonathan, as if he had guessed David's wish. He slashed his arm below the sleeve of his tunic. Blood reddened his fingers.

David recovered the knife and made a similar wound, and they mingled their blood in the ancient and irreversible rite which makes brothers of enemies and lovers of friends. They bound each other's wounds, and exchanged their tunics—Jonathan's green for David's blue—and David said:

"My friends shall be your friends, and my enemies shall be your enemies, and neither man nor woman, whether mother, father, brother, sister, wife, or child, shall come before you. Let Ashtoreth bear witness that we honor her above all other deities. Let Yahweh bear witness that we do not swear our love to spite him, but in spite of him. So said my ancestress Ruth, the woman of Moab: 'Where thou diest, will I die, and there will be buried: The Lord do so to me, and more also, if ought but death part thee and me.'"

David watched him depart among the flowers, and sometimes they hid him, and sometimes his golden head seemed a moving flower, and once he turned and called:

"David."

"Yes, Jonathan?"

"If I went with you—"

"If you went with me—"

"I would not be the Jonathan you love."

Crows screamed raucously into the sky behind him and David thought, Thus are the people Jonathan leaves with me. Except Abraham. Yes, even Michal. Then he was ashamed by so heartless a thought and the poet's soul of him conjured a kinder image:

Daisies are little folk, the shepherds and farmers. Sunflowers are princes and princesses who bend toward their father, the sun, their faces reflecting his light, but warmed no more by the sun above them than by the daisies at their feet.

But the sun may hide behind clouds or even set, and the sunflowers break their stalks, the daisies be trampled by wolves, and one of them cry, "Where is our father, the sun?"

There were no sunflowers where David fled from Saul, the long, desperate flight which led him eventually to Achish

and his Philistines and to the fortress city of Ziklag, where
he must wait and watch while the people of his birth and
the people who had sheltered him prepared for the ultimate
war and the rising of a new sun.

Chapter

TWELVE

He looked as if he had climbed from Sheol. Muffled and
stooped, he stumbled into the tent and she caught him in
her arms; she, Rizpah, who had supplanted his queen. He
did not tell her where he had been on this night before the
battle; he did not need to tell her that he had visited the
Witch of Endor in spite of his own edict and asked her the
dreaded question: Will Israel crush Philistia at Mt. Gilboa?

"Has my lord heard ill tidings?" she asked, skillfully re-
moving his sandals and robe, easing him onto the couch,
pouring a cup of pomegranate wine from a leather flagon.
Stupid Rizpah; pathetic Rizpah; she laughed when she heard
men speak of her in such terms. She—she with her spies,
Elim and the rest—and not Ahinoam or Michal was the
strongest woman in Israel. It was she who had urged the king
to destroy David. It was she who had urged him to forgive
and recall Jonathan, "lest he join David and alienate your
people, for he is greatly loved."

"I have heard the mutterings of a foolish young woman,"
said Saul, with the petulance of a child. "She conjures a
ghost and calls him Samuel. And yet I removed my sandals
and knelt before him like a simple shepherd, and trembled
before his wrath!"

"Did you not know his face?"

"I saw a shrouded old man who, for all I knew, was the
witch's own grandfather, or the witch herself, deceiving my
ears and my eyes with her black arts. I was right to banish
such people. I will see to her after the battle."

She liked to see him angry and spirited, like the lion of

Israel in the days of his pride, when emissaries from Egypt had knelt before him with gifts of ivory and gold, and the king of Tyre had sent him a hundred tunics of Tyrian purple for the officers of his growing army. But she was deeply troubled that he treated his visit to the Witch of Endor with suspicion and disdain. The Witch was neither a novice nor a charlatan. The people called her a sister to Ahinoam, for they greatly resembled each other except in the color of their hair and neither had aged perceptibly since they came to Israel from Caphtor. Samuel—and she did not doubt that Saul had truly seen him—must have foretold defeat. She felt as if a Lilith fumbled at her throat. But she dared not reveal such forebodings to Saul. With Rizpah, concealment and dissimulation had become genius.

"The Witch of Endor is a woman with a pretty face and dyed hair and no more power than I to conjure the dead. Let my lord sleep and refresh himself for the battle tomorrow."

"Call Jonathan to me."

"Would you wake him so late, my lord?" She did not want to share her lover before the battle. She wanted to cradle him in her arms and possess him utterly, if perhaps for the last time. He was her Abraham, he was her Moses, yes, he was more to her than Yahweh or the gods of Ammon, and her devious and calculating mind, her aging body, served him with singlehearted devotion.

"You know he never sleeps before a battle."

The prince was quickly summoned and quick to appear.

"My son," Saul said, "I think the same demons are besetting both of us. Yet we shall need our strength tomorrow."

"It will be as it has always been," said Jonathan, beardless and young as when he had first met David, though his eyes had turned gray when David went into exile and people said of him, "The sea has gone out of his face." But the wild chrysanthemums of Elah still burned in his hair.

"But David was with us once. What if he comes against you in the battle tomorrow? For three years I pursued him in the Wilderness. For three more years he has served the Philistines."

"He will not fight against his own people."

"But if he should? You, you, Jonathan. If you should

meet him in the fray, his arm upraised to strike you with his sword?"

"Then I would kneel and receive his blow and bless him with my last breath."

Saul looked at him with a long, pitying look. There had been a time when he would have shrieked in rage or hurled a spear. Now he said without bitterness:

"If we win the battle, perhaps you will tell me about David, whom you love above your father and your king. I have loved two women. One brought me pain, one brought me peace. I regret neither. I loved David too as a son. And you most of all. But the love between men which passes friendship—"

"It cannot be told," said Jonathan. "Except that it isn't a sin to those who so love. It came into the world, I think, when the Lady first walked among men. 'Let there be love,' she said. She did not say, 'Let there be love only between a man and a maid or a son and his father.'"

"Ah, the Goddess. I have served only Yahweh, but he has forsaken me. Perhaps I have judged her ill, and those are wise who have served her as well as a god."

"David and I, my father."

"Perhaps David will come back to us."

"You would call him back?" cried Jonathan. "You would forgive him, Father? He was never disloyal to you."

"It is almost light," said Rizpah. "And David, I think, will indeed be with those who march against us tomorrow."

Gilboa, though often called a mount, was a ridge of lime-stone hills instead of a single peak; hills like those where Saul and his army, for twenty years, had outfought the Philistines, leaping from crag to crag like wild ibexes, laughing at the heavy armor which encumbered the enemy and the stones which splintered the spokes in their chariot wheels. Now, for the first time, the five great Philistine cities had met as one nation and assembled the largest army ever to march against Israel, with numberless chariots hammered of bronze and iron and armor no sword could pierce. Saul and Jonathan silently surveyed the tents which empurpled the plain like deadly mushrooms; turned and faced each other; and embraced as father and son for the first time in many years.

"I know why David loves you," Saul said, and the words were like hemlock poured into Rizpah's ear; she was no longer first. "You are one of those golden angels which Yahweh sent to Abraham to tell him that Sarah at ninety would bear him another child. You fight for me and Israel. And yet you would rather build gardens with David. Or stand on the shores of the Great Green Sea and count the dolphins. And who can say you are wrong? I only know that I have greatly wronged you, whom I love the best." Then in turn he embraced his younger sons, Ahinidab and Machishua, beardless youths who had never fought a war; strong with a plow, clumsy with a spear. But, being ignorant of Philistines, they were eager to fight. Rizpah, momentarily ignored (how often ignored!), stood behind them when Ahinoam, their mother, came from her tent to embrace them and cling lovingly to Jonathan. Ahinoam did not know of Saul's visit to the Witch of Endor, but she turned to Saul and said:

"The Philistines have surely learned our ways by now. I fear for you, my lord. I think you should scout the hills behind you."

It was such a remark as Rizpah would never have made to Saul. A woman advising a king before a battle!

Saul frowned and said, "I have set men to guard the principal passes into the hills. Only ignorant shepherds know the bypaths."

"Yahweh go with you then." She did not mention the Lady, nor did she remind him that he had failed to sacrifice to any god; that he had been estranged from Yahweh since the death of Samuel.

He looked at her with sudden tenderness. "And the Lady as well?"

"The Lady as well. Even Yahweh acknowledges her power. Or why do his priests so often revile her?"

"You can never forget her, can you? Nor the island of the sunken palaces."

He kissed her tenderly on the mouth. He accepts defeat, thought Rizpah. Otherwise, he would not debase me before his discarded queen.

"If only you had been less beautiful! If only a little gray had sprinkled your hair! It is not easy to grow old in the company of a goddess. Why, to look at you makes me wish

I were still that bold young man beside the well in Endor!"
Then, remembering Rizpah and drawing her to his side, he
said, "Come, my sons. It is time to march. Rizpah will send
us on our way."

Thus he returned to being a king and a general of twenty
years, except that now he was old and tired and would rather
return to his farm than lead an outnumbered army against
a foe he could no longer hate. He is not mad, thought Rizpah.
He will not forget his commands or sulk in his tent; he is
resigned. David is not with him. All that I wanted I won, but
at what a cost! I wanted Saul and took him from Ahinoam.
I envied David's power and drove him into flight. Yet here
today, I must confront myself and my chosen fate: fruition
or drought; the delectable figs of Sharon or the wizened
apples of the Dead Sea Valley.

The day she had first met Saul, when he had come to her,
an aging harlot in newly conquered Ammon, she had stared
at him, straight and kingly then but starting to gray, and
thought: It is not a queen he needs. He is tired of Ahinoam's
beauty, her mind, her pride. It is comfort he needs, a hood
instead of a crown; gray robes instead of purple; and I will
command the highest arts of my trade into winning his love.

"My lord Saul is weary," she had said. "Let me anoint his
feet with the balm of Gilead. . . ." And she had loved him
to her triumph and now, at the last, to her despair.

And what of David? At first she had liked the boy. He won
victories for Israel. He was quick, kind, and intelligent. He
sang for Saul and treated her like a queen instead of a concubine. But then the maidens sang at the wells, "Saul has
slain his thousands. David his ten thousands." She felt the
scorpion sting of jealousy. Saul was her lover, Saul was her
lord. Surpassed by a shepherd from little Bethlehem? Why,
the boy would demand the throne!

"David and Jonathan are building a garden," she had said
at a carefully chosen time, when Saul was taking his ease
from the midday heat in an upper chamber of his palace.
She knelt beside his couch, fanning him with a fan of ivory
and peacock feathers.

"A garden?" asked Saul with interest, no doubt remembering his youth. "A good thing indeed. We have need of fruits
and vegetables for the palace."

"Indeed. And their friendship is beautiful to watch as they

work together. David, I think, will always serve you because of his love for Jonathan. Why, even now I have seen them pause in their work and whisper together and kiss on the lips like a man and a maid, though which was the maid I cannot say—they are both such valiant warriors—and crown each other with flowers."

Thus had she planted the oleander seeds of suspicion: forbidden love and treason against the throne. Thus had she separated Jonathan from his father and rid the court of David.

But now she must send her beloved into battle, a tired old man, white of beard like Abraham, gaunt and guilty like Jonah fleeing the Lord, more dear to her than in his lordly prime. He had pitched his camp in the lower hills of Gilboa, above and to the side of the plain where the armies would meet. He had left a sufficient guard—except in the case of total rout—and Rizpah was not afraid for her life. She did not want to live if Saul should die, but she wanted desperately for him to live and return to his farm with her for their final years.

She watched the Israelites march from the camp in their tattered, deadly ranks—this man armored, that man clad in a goatskin, this man carrying a spear, that man a staff. Foot soldiers, climbers, leapers, archers, slingers . . . the roughest, most ill-equipped army between Egypt and Assyria, the only large army without chariots, and till now the most feared. Its departure seemed to Rizpah like the receding of a great tide (though she had never seen the sea), and she earnestly prayed to Yahweh and the Ammonite Baal for its return.

Ahinoam took her hand. "Let us go forth to watch our lord smite the foe."

To watch your precious Jonathan, Rizpah thought. What do you care for Saul, you brazen witch! But she did not remove the unwelcome hand. She envied Ahinoam: her beauty, her grace, the power she held over Saul, and because to the country Ahinoam remained the Queen while she, Rizpah, was a bedraggled whore who had stolen the Queen's bed. But it was well to maintain a pretense of friendliness, since Saul in his way still loved his queen. She pressed Ahinoam's hand. The small perfect fingers as always made her feel plain and clumsy and old, but she would not have traded Saul for Ahinoam's beauty, no, not even for Jonathan as a son.

They found a vantage point atop a crag—weeds to prickle their knees through their woolen robes and a frightened cony to keep them company—and watched the Israelites not so much arrayed as scattered across the plain, awaiting the attack. The Philistine army advanced in a movement called the Bladed Square. First the swordsmen, each carrying two spears and a short sword of lethal iron. Then the archers, who fired their arrows over the heads of the swordsmen. Then a second row of swordsmen to protect the archers when they had exhausted their quivers. Finally the ox-drawn wagons which would fall to the Israelites in case of defeat. They lumbered into battle because they contained supplies and physicians and, more important, massive images of the fish-tailed Dagon, the luck of the army, as the Ark of the Tabernacle had been the luck of the Israelites before its capture by the Philistines. Chariots and horsemen rode beside the square to prevent a flanking attack. Such an army was almost impervious on a flat terrain, for every chariot contained a driver and a swordsman, protected by an armored cowl, and battle knives had been affixed to the wheels to mutilate foot soldiers who attacked the charioteers and tried to drag them from their chariots.

The shrill blast of a ram's horn rebounded among the hills, and scarcely had it sunk into silence than the Israelite archers unloosed a barrage of arrows, which swished and shrilled in the air like deadly eagles. The Philistines raised their oval bronze shields against the assault. A few of the arrows struck below the shields at unprotected feet or at legs protected only by finely meshed greaves. There were cries of anger and pain and the crash of a chariot which had lost its horses. But the Israelites were not experienced archers; with their thin leather shields, they did not wait to receive a returning volley but turned and, quick as conies, scuttled among the hills. It was not a retreat, it was the traditional planned withdrawal, executed with a speed which in the past had never failed to surprise an army laden with armor and accustomed to set battles.

"He has not lost his skill," Rizpah cried. "Have you ever seen such speed?"

"Rizpah," Ahinoam gasped, pointing to the Philistine host.

Two new champions had joined the enemy.

They were taller by three heads than the tallest Philistines. Their armor was so prodigious that any normal man would have stumbled beneath its weight. The two brothers of Goliath, stricken by demons of fever before Michmash, indeed, later presumed dead, had reappeared to fight with the enemy.

A voice like that of Baal, the Thunderer, broke the silence. "Israelites, where is your David with his slingshot now?"

Rizpah, Ahinoam, Saul—none of the Israelites except possibly Jonathan knew the whereabouts of David, who had fled from Saul for three years in the wilderness and finally accepted Achish's offer to rule Ziklag. He had steadfastly refused to fight against his own people. He had fought the Bedouins and kept them from harassing the caravans which plied between Egypt, Philistia, and Phoenicia. He had grown a beard as red and flamboyant as his hair and, when Saul announced that Michal was no longer David's wife, promptly married a certain Abigail, a rich and beautiful widow whom poets likened to a vineyard ripe with grapes and wooed by bees. He was a hero to the Israelites because he had never raised his hand against the king who had tried to kill him. Not yet, because of Jonathan. Today, however, when Yahweh and Ashtoreth, it seemed, had joined battle, the god of mountain and sky, the goddess of earth and sea, would he fight for generous masters against an ungenerous king?

The army of Israel paused in its flight to stare at these one-eyed ghosts of Goliath, no less tall and terrible, and doubtless remembered the shepherd boy who had killed the giant. Everyone knew that, before his death, Samuel had anointed David king over Israel. Everyone knew that Saul had refused to sacrifice to Yahweh before the battle. Had Goliath's brothers been sent to punish him?

Rizpah shrieked and began to wave her arms at the distant figure of Saul. "Fly into the hills! There the giants will flounder among the rocks!"

"Hush, Rizpah. He can't hear you. Don't you see what is happening? There, above us . . . ?"

High in the hills, a movement among the rocks, a man, men, advancing on silent feet; high in the hills which the legless Dagon had made his sea.

"Our men, surely."

"No. Their helmets bear purple crests." The Philistines never fought without their crests; such was their pride. Purple was Dagon color, murex color, sea color.

The ridges of Gilboa were aswarm with Philistines. Someone had shown them the secret passes into the hills which only "ignorant shepherds know."

Like a blacksmith holding a horseshoe between his tongs, they held the Israelites between the main army below them and the climbers above them. And the Israelites had not climbed high enough to escape the chariots, which clambered up the slopes like giant crabs: new chariots, wheels of iron instead of bronze, grinding wheels which stones could not break, but which broke men's legs like enormous claws.

Saul, beleaguered, fought like a wounded lion. Embattled Jonathan struggled to reach his side.

"David has betrayed us," said Rizpah dully. "He has shown the Philistines to the secret passes. He has murdered my lord."

"David or another, and he has murdered my son." Ahinoam had seen the Cyclops' arrow in Jonathan's breast.

Chapter

THIRTEEN

The lost battle reechoed in his brain: the brazen chariots as they stormed the slopes, the bladed wheels as they slashed the wild grasses and the legs of men; the eagle-shrill of arrows; the lightning of spears. Gilboa had come to life and treacherously devoured his mountain-dwelling people. The cruel and unrelenting sun had sparkled the blotches of blood on the plain, and he, David, the exile of Israel, had watched his people routed and overrun; Jonathan felled with an arrow, Saul as he fell on his sword.

After dark, when the slopes lay hushed with their burden of death, he had dared the lions and hyenas in search of life; in search of Jonathan or Jonathan's body. He was not surprised when a hooded figure approached him across the field.

He knew the queen behind the faltering gait, the hidden face. The sweetness of her in the midst of death affronted his nostrils; finally she groped for words.

"David, my son, they have taken the bodies of Saul and Jonathan and his brothers from the field. I could not stop them."

He fell to his knees with inarticulate grief. He raised his face to the blank and unresponsive moon, to the heedless mountain, and sobbed a lament for his own comfort and for the unlamented dead. He wanted to stop his ears and hide from Ahinoam as from a demented leper. Life in a field of death was doubly cruel. She had no right to glitter even in the dark, unsmashed beauty amid the ruins.

"You saw the battle?" he said at last.

"I waited with Rizpah on a neighboring crag. I watched them die, Saul and his sons. Jonathan too, the princeliest of them all. We returned to the camp. We fled with the slaves and servants when the Philistines overran us. Rizpah was captured. I hid in a cave with a fox which never moved but stared at me with terrible eyes, the eyes of death. It was your anguish which called to me across the night and I came—not to succor you, for what have I left to give?— but to share, I think, the burden of grief. Perhaps divided it will be endurable. David, my son, was it you who showed the Philistines the secret passes behind Gilboa?"

Sadly he shook his head. "It was not by choice. The Philistines were kind to me, and Achish became my friend. We talked of ships and voyages and the Island of Green Magic, your home. We talked of inconsequential things, never of war. He did not ask me to betray my own people. But once I told him of hunting a lion on the slopes of Gilboa. How I had climbed a secret path which the shepherds knew and surprised the beast in his lair. Achish remembered, and thus only did I betray my people."

"I believe you, David. You are not to blame for Gilboa, nor even Saul and his madness. It was Yahweh, I think, who forsook his people. And how could the Lady help them? Sometimes they pray to her, but the Philistines build her temples and honor her priests. I believe that she stood apart and wept for both of the armies, but more for Israel. But now we must find the bodies and bury them with proper rites or they will be homeless ghosts throughout eternity."

"Is Ashtoreth so cruel?"

"It is Yahweh who rules the dead of Israel, though he has lost the living."

"Isn't he satisfied with the blood he has wrought?"

"Sometimes the gods obey a law beyond themselves, the Mother of the Mother, the Father of the Father. Sometimes it is we ourselves who bring on our heads the whirlwind we call the gods. The beauty of Israel is slain upon its high places. That is what history will say, and that is all."

He did not like speech at such a time. Silence was harsh; speech was intolerable. He must act upon her words.

"How shall we know where the Philistines have taken them?"

"Alecto, the Siren, will know. We are close to Endor. We shall seek her now."

"But you are a Siren, Ahinoam. Where are your powers?"

"I put them from me when I married Saul, or hid them and let them die. Some remained. I can speak to the living without speech and hear the unspoken language of their hearts. I can call to a bird on the wing or summon a dolphin out of the deeps. But the dead are beyond me."

He walked in a dream and Ahinoam walked beside him, the queen of unshed tears. She looked at him searchingly and gave him her hand for support (it was he, not she, who staggered, like one with the gift of tongues).

"David, it is I who have brought you grief. It was I who sent you to Jonathan. How could I not have guessed that he would encircle you in his doom? For he was too beautiful to live in this world of toiling shadows."

"Jonathan was my god," he said. "Not Yahweh, nor Ashtoreth. He was the bread which I broke at the festival, he was the vintage rich from the treading feet. Would you have wished me godless and songless? All of the days of my life, though I move as a ghost, I will move in grace because I loved him."

They came at last to Endor and found the house of Alecto, the sun-dried bricks with the spindly wooden staircase climbing to the roof. David pounded her door with impatient fists.

When Alecto opened the door, she was garbed in simple green homespun and wearing a single small tourmaline on her smallest finger. She had not aged, but she had grieved; her sea-green eyes were dim with tears.

"Ahinoam and David," she said. "I have been expecting you. Come quickly into the house. There are still Philistines in the town."

Net entwining shells; couch made of oars; the figurehead of a ship: Here were the voyages which he might have taken with Jonathan. ("You may voyage to foreign lands in search of apes and ivory, frankincense and nard. . . .")

He must speak or weep. "They say you can raise the dead. Is it true, Alecto, Siren and Witch of Endor?"

"Men call me a witch because I tell them the truth. Yes, I can raise the dead. The ghosts of Sheol, for they are restless beings, shadows and therefore lonely. I raised the spirit of Samuel before the battle. But the happy spirits of the Celestial Vineyard will not—cannot—answer me."

"Can you summon my friend Jonathan?"

"He was a loving boy. He may have attained the Celestial Vineyard."

"His wings were too small, I think. Will you call to him?"

Alecto's eyes held conquests and civilizations, burning towers and ravished princesses; the wrath of kings and the infidelity of queens whose beauty had kindled wars. He did not find in her the civilizing compassion of Ahinoam. The elemental moods of the sea still strove in her; its sudden fury and halcyon calm, the laughter of dolphins, the sinister scything of sharks. Only the Goddess could command her. Only to those she liked would she be kind. Perhaps she approved him; perhaps she accepted him for Ahinoam's sake.

"Mama, who are these men?"

A small child, asleep and unnoticed in a bed of tortoise-shell, had awakened to peer at them with sleepy eyes. A spray of garlic hung above his bed to protect him from Walk-Behinders and other demons, who might wish to steal him and leave a changeling in his place, for he was a radiant child, with eyes like the sea at the edge of the world and hair as yellow as corn.

"They are my friends," she said. "They were your father's friends."

Ahinoam looked at David with disbelief. "I did not know. For once I did not read his heart."

"He did not know himself. It is Jonathan's child, however. We came here together once."

"And he loved me," Alecto said, "for the little space of a

night. But the night was a tender moon and a field of chrysanthemums."

"I am glad," said Ahinoam. "He has left a part of himself in a world diminished by his departure." She bent to lift the child from his bed.

"Please," said Alecto. "The Philistines sacked the village before you came. They did not hurt me, nor steal my things, because they knew me to be a Siren. But they frightened Mephibosheth. He fled to his couch, but fell and hurt his knee. You must not touch him except to kiss his cheek."

"You mustn't fear the Philistines, Mephibosheth," said David. "They are my friends and I will protect you from them."

"And Walk-Behinders. What about them?"

"I killed a giant with a sling, and he was fiercer than any demon there is!"

"My father is not coming back, is he? Mama told me a long time ago."

"A month ago," she whispered. "It seems an eternity to him. He thinks his father is a great king in a distant kingdom who cannot leave his people."

"And so he would have been," said David. "Come now, Alecto. Let us speak to him."

She will garb herself in the habiliments of a seeress, he thought, the hood and the black robe. She will fall to her knees or sacrifice a goat.

But she had no need for such empty trappings; she, a Siren.

"Sit here beside me on the couch and hold my hands," she said, a beautiful maiden with arms which were whiter than the whitest lamb. Whether the room grew dark, he did not know. Rather it seemed to him that he was taken to a place of darkness where the voice of Alecto—he could not see her face—rang like a bell on a distant buoy.

"Lady of the Wild Things, Lady of Love," Alecto whispered, "grieve for a grieving mother and a friend who was more than a brother. Make of their grief a monument to love and raise the spirit of Jonathan, prince of Israel, from the netherland which is Sheol."

He had waited before a battle with fear upon him. He had waited before he met Goliath with a horror of timelessness, with the feeling that Joshua had stopped the sun and every water clock had ceased to drip. It was worse in this land with no name. *He will not come. The old magic is dead. No more does Ahinoam swim in the Great Green Sea nor Alecto sit on the rocks and comb her labyrinthine hair, nor Jonathan ride the dolphins. No more does the terebinth tree enfold its house as if it were a nest against the storm. Like a plague of darkness, the time of the Cyclops has fallen upon the land, and where is Joshua to recover the sun?*

Mephibosheth took his hand and said in a small, brave voice, "I came too, David." He limped in a linen robe which fell to his feet, hiding his wounded knee, and each little foot thrust back and forth, back and forth, like the feelers of a snail. In his free hand, he carried a lamp like an opening chrysanthemum.

"Mama told you she would try to call my father. I heard her. I wasn't asleep at all. I want to see him too."

"But how can we find him, Mephibosheth?" David cried, clasping the child's hand.

"I will call his name. Maybe he will hear us. Papa, it is I, Mephibosheth, and David, your friend. Help us to find you, for we have lost our way!"

In a place without stars, in a place without name, Jonathan came to them out of the white dusk, parting the mist as one parts the flaps to a tent. An arrow clutched at his chest and blood cobwebbed his face.

"Jonathan, my brother, can you hear me?"

"I can hear you, David, but I cannot see your face."

"Your son is with me. It was he who called to you."

"Is it well with you, my son?"

"Yes, Papa, so long as you speak to me."

"David is your father now. Look after him as if he were me. He is sometimes sad and you must be like a cricket on his hearth, singing a merry tune to make him laugh."

"I will do that, Papa."

"What is this place?" David asked.

"No-Land, wherever that may be. Yahweh has not forgiven my love for you. He has barred me from Sheol."

David grasped for his hand and his fingers closed on air.

"Perhaps the Goddess will help you reach the Vineyard."

Jonathan's smile, ineffably sweet, unspeakably sad, was like a stone from a sling in David's breast. "My wings are memories. How shall they lift me out of this well of night? Even the air is a wet embrace."

"Ashtoreth," David pleaded, lifting his arms toward a sky which he could not see. "At least let us touch him, Mephibosheth and me!"

Momentarily the shadow held shape and substance, the dear configurations of the beloved, and David grasped his arm.

"David, David, I can see you at last and feel the warmth of your hand. And you, my son. My two blankets against the cold. David, it was a happy time we had together at Elah and Gibeah."

"It was not enough," shouted David. "What is a world without Jonathan?"

"The world must be ruled. Who but my friend, anointed by Samuel, shall rally the scattered armies of Israel?"

Form melted into mist, mist eddied into white and estranging dark.

"Jonathan, wait for me. How shall I find you again?"

"Recover my body and that of my father and brothers from the temple to Dagon at Beth-Shan and give us decent burial. Perhaps you will find a sign. . . ."

He sat on a couch between the two women, in the cramped room, in the cramped world. Mephibosheth lay in his bed looking at them with large green eyes.

"I saw him," said Ahinoam. "He smiled and spoke and reached out his hand to me. But I could not even touch him. And you, David?"

"Mephibosheth was with me. Even Yahweh has no quarrel with a child. Both of us held him for a little moment. Alecto, can you raise him again?"

Sadly she shook her head. "It is not possible. Now you must let him rest. Sleep is the only blessing left to him."

David embraced her and smelled the salt from the sea. "If Samuel's prophecy should come to pass that the anointed should rule"—he could not bring himself to speak his own name—"then the witch and the sorcerer will once again be welcome in Israel."

"He is in Sheol?" Ahinoam asked uncertainly. "I could not be sure."

"He is in No-Land," said David. "It is worse than Sheol. There aren't even shadows to keep him company."

"David, David, what shall we do?" The old eyes in the young face besought his answer. Her question deferred to his strength, but he felt like a lost and forsaken child. She, she should know every answer to every question. She was the queen, she was the Siren, immortal of beauty, powerful even in ruin.

"He told me to find Saul's body and those of his sons and give them decent burial. They are in Beth-Shan."

"Nailed to the walls of a temple." She shuddered. "It is the Philistine way. But how can we enter an enemy town without an army?"

"The Philistines are drunk with their victory. No one will think to guard the bodies."

"We cannot go alone. We cannot carry the bodies."

"When he first became king, your husband defended the town of Jabesh-Gilead against the army of Nahash, the Ammonite. The people swore fealty to Saul and his descendants. They fought with him gallantly in his last battle, but some, no doubt, escaped and fled with Abner among the hills. They will doubtless retreat to their high-walled town. Let us go there now and ask their help."

The walk was long and difficult; a Night Stalker flew at Ahinoam out of a tamarisk tree and David beat him to death with his bare fists and cast him at her feet. All of the night and all of the following day they walked toward Jabesh-Gilead, the city as old as Cain; sometimes they hid in caves or hovels from the marauding Philistines. There was little to steal in the huts of the Israelites, and the beauty of Israelite women, dark and voluptuous, was not to the taste of the victors, but victory was wine to them and drunkenness made them cruel. Ahinoam hid her gold beneath a rustic's robe, and David dyed his hair with the brown ocher from the banks of a stream. Sometimes the natives knew them by the way they walked, or the way David moved his arms, with rapid, sure motions, always the slinger, or the way Ahinoam never lowered her eyes, even to face the sun, and gave them provisions and water until they came at last to Jabesh-Gilead, which, like a grim but kindly spirit, guarded a fertile valley of vineyards and olive trees. The town was wracked by grief over Israel's loss, but Ahinoam and David, though kingdomless, were greeted like a queen and a prince.

"We bring danger with us," David was prompt to confess. "The Philistines have turned against me because I would not fight with them against Israel, and they would like to lead Ahinoam in chains through Gaza and Askelon."

The answer was unequivocal. "We have our walls. We remember Saul."

Ahinoam smiled with the old artless witchery of her youth. "You do us honor, my faithful friends. Yet we have more to ask. Listen to David's plan."

"You owe me nothing," said David. "After my wanderings in the desert, I served the Philistines for three years. I dined with Achish, the seren of Gath, and ruled in Ziklag."

"You are not to blame. It was Saul who hounded you through the wilderness and into the arms of the foe."

"Nor was he to blame. His demon drove him to madness. Will you help me recover his body and that of his sons from the walls of Beth-Shan?"

Without exception the people of the town—and surely the smallest child to the oldest graybeard had gathered to greet these famous exiles—agreed to the plan. It was as if slaves had discarded their chains or cowards had discovered courage. At least a hundred warriors pleaded to join the group, even an old one-legged man on crutches who remembered Deborah; the women encouraged their husbands and sons and promised to offer Yahweh a sacrifice of thirty cattle and sixty sheep, a costly gift for so poor a town.

But David sought valor and not numbers. It was hard to find men who had not been wounded on the slopes of Gilboa. But finally he chose his band—ten of them—not so much for their strength as for a look in their eyes which seemed to say: "We have fought much but not too much. For Jonathan, the pride of Israel, we would fight the Giants of Gath!" After he had made his choice—and they were quick to answer the famous David of the red hair and rapid arm—he spoke in a quiet firm voice:

"We will all wear tunics like soldiers and shave our cheeks and trust to the night and the drunkenness of the victors. May Yahweh walk with us." (The Goddess was little worshipped in Jabesh-Gilead, but Ahinoam whispered to David, "And I will plead with the Lady and shear the locks from my head.")

Ahinoam took his face between her hands and kissed him on the mouth.

"If I were a man, I would fight at your side," she said. "Bring back my husband's body. He loved the earth—seed-time, harvest, and haying—and therefore I loved him, though he was called to the wars against his will and finally came to like them." (She did not reproach him for Rizpah.) "Bring back my sons to me, and the son whom I loved the best. Once, when you fought Goliath, I hurled green magic against him. I have no magic to send with you now—except my love of the Lady."

"I will do as you say," said David, loving her because she was a great queen who made a splendor of exile and an exaltation of grief; because, like the simplest farmer's wife, she must suffer the loss of her husband and sons; and because she was Jonathan's mother. To look at her you would have thought that she had slept on eiderdown and stepped, fragrant and glistening, from her bath. Honey Hair! But David had passed beyond desire or awe; to him she was his second friend.

Distances were short, even if difficult and often pathless, in Israel. It was a single day's walk to Beth-Shan. But the Philistines had overrun the countryside like a plague of flies. No one questioned David and his men. Except for David, they were shorter and shaggier than most Philistines, their features were aquiline, their skin and hair dark. They were farmers and herdsmen who worked in the fields by day and returned to their huts in Jabesh-Gilead only at night; they were not of the sea or the city. But some of the Israelites had fought for Philistia as mercenaries; such seemed David and his men, and no one attempted to question them. David, already brown of hair, smeared his tunic with dirt and blood like a veteran of Gilboa and hid his face with a hood.

Beth-Shan was enkindled with torches and riotous with merrymakers. The garrison was small; the priests more numerous than soldiers. It was a sacred town, a town of temples to Dagon and Ashtoreth, and no enemy had presumed to attack its low and indefensible walls, not even the Israelites, who, though they execrated Dagon even above Baal, secretly honored the Lady.

No one questioned them as they entered the gate, between

the two stone images, one of fish-tailed Dagon with the face and arms of a man, the other of Ashtoreth cradling fruit in her arms.

They followed the revelers to the temple of Dagon. The Israelites did not build temples to Yahweh—they worshipped him at an altar of clumsily piled stones or under the spreading limbs of a sacred tree. Philistine temples were foreign to them. Red, swelling columns, blue walls, flat roofs covered with decorative tiles . . . porticoes and altars of chiseled green marble . . . courtyards where maidens danced the slow, shuffling Dance of the Crane . . . priests with shaven heads, the young in loincloths, the old in robes which reached to their ankles: these were the echoes of Crete which honored the fish-tailed god.

The body of Saul had been nailed to the wall by his hands, and his severed head had been raised on a stake at his feet. His younger sons by Ahinoam, Ahinidab and Machishua, also slain in the battle, hung beside him. Only Jonathan was not with them; the Philistines had respected him even in death; they doubtless knew that he was not Saul's son; they did not wish or perhaps they feared to dismember a Siren's son. They had bound him by leather straps to a column of Ashtoreth's temple. Except for the blood on his face, he was as white as the salt flats around the Dead Sea, and sad in sleep, as if he were haunted by dreams. But death, like a lover, had left him beautiful.

Philistine soldiers were hurling clods of earth at the head of Saul. His features were blurred beyond recognition. The eyes were gone, the gray hair was clotted with blood.

They were making sport of him with words as well as blows. The Philistines taught their children by questions and answers known as Wisdoms. It was a form which they could raise to an art or lower to a curse.

"Where is your crown, oh king of Israel who would drive us into the sea? Where are the shepherds who sleep beneath the sky and wield their staves instead of their swords?"

"On Gilboa," the answer rang. "Ask the vultures to show you the way."

"Where is Rizpah, harlot of Israel?"

"Seek her in chains beside the unchanging sea."

Hatred burned in David like the poison of wild gourds. It was not of the gods, whatever men said, this thing which drove them to fight and kill and exult. Or else it was Hate, and men should raise him a temple or heap him an altar of stones. David must fight him now or leap on the revelers' backs as if they were a pride of lions. But reason restrained him, the weir which checked the turbulence of his nature. He remembered the similar cruelties of the Israelites. He had seen them conquer a town, massacre women along with men, children along with mothers.

"We will wait now," he said. "The Philistines will soon exhaust themselves and sleep. Let us pretend to join them. Sing and dance and reel in the streets, and pretend to hurl clay at our king. But drink neither wine nor beer. Our time will come."

The Lady Moon descended the heavens, slowly, slowly, as if she wished to illumine the merrymaking (she was much honored by the Philistines, who mistook her for Ashtoreth; but the Goddess would close her eyes upon such a sight). The cries of merriment dwindled to a low, murmurous titter, then into such a silence as follows a battle, whether defeat or victory. Men fell asleep in their tracks and slid to the earth, friend leaned against friend. Mongrels, a cat, a goat prowled through the streets in search of food but kept their distance from the sleeping men.

"Now," said David.

The bodies were strangely light; Saul seemed an ancient scarecrow, the sons beside him like little children. They had lost much blood. There was an odor of death about them, like the damp and decay in a cellar of moldering bones. Except Jonathan. The wild grasses of Gilboa had cloaked him in a green fragrance. With infinite tenderness, without the help of his friends, David lowered his body to the ground. (*No one shall touch him but me. No one shall be his blanket against the cold.*)

They borrowed robes from the sleepers to hide the bodies. Nobody stopped them as they left the town. A drowsy guard at the gate nodded good night.

"Too much beer?" he mumbled, pointing to the shrouded bodies.

"Yes, that and the battle."

"They'll be drinking beer from Gaza to Bethlehem tomorrow!" he chortled.

In a forest beyond Beth-Shan, they threaded litters of

willow wands and carried their burden for most of the night.

"Stop here and rest," said David in a grove of palms and tamarisks, beside a well with crumbling walls and an old copper bucket on a rusted chain. The men dipped water and drank and stretched wearily on their robes and slept the sleep of the dead. The water was clean and cold. The wind made lyre notes in the swaying fronds.

David leaned his back against a tree, unable to sleep, with Jonathan's head in his lap. Like most of his people, he had no fear of death; he had fought too many battles. It did not even seem to him that Jonathan was dead.

"Little brother," he said. "You were older than I. You taught me how to fight. But I grew taller than you in the wilderness, and at the last it was I you needed to shield you from the giant. I should have taken the arrow in my breast."

And David sang:

"The beauty of Israel is slain upon thy high places:
How are the mighty fallen!
Tell it not in Gath,
Publish it not in the streets of Askelon;
Lest the daughters of the Philistines rejoice,
Lest the daughters of the uncircumcised triumph.
Ye mountains of Gilboa, let there be no dew,
Neither let there be rain, upon you,
Nor fields of offerings; for there the shield of
          the Mighty
Is vilely cast away,
The shield of Saul, as though he had not been
          anointed with oil.

From the blood of the slain,
From the fat of the mighty,
The bow of Jonathan turned not back,
And the sword of Saul returned not empty.
Saul and Jonathan were lovely and pleasant in
          their lives,
And in their death they were not divided:
They were swifter than eagles,
They were stronger than lions.
Ye daughters of Israel, weep over Saul,
Who clothed you in scarlet, with other delights,
Who put on ornaments of gold upon your apparel.

How are the mighty fallen in the midst of the battle!
O Jonathan, thou wast slain in thine high places.
I am distressed for thee, my brother Jonathan:
Very pleasant hast thou been unto me:
Thy love to me was wonderful, passing the love of
        women.
How are the mighty fallen,
And the weapons of war perished."

He lifted Jonathan lightly in his arms and laid him on the grass beside the well. He raised a bucket of water and, tearing a linen strip from his own tunic, bathed the blood from Jonathan's face and started to bind the arrow wound in his chest. He turned the body in his lap, as one might turn a baby to sprinkle him with myrrh. Only then did he see the hunched and swollen back beneath the cloth.

"They have crippled you!" he cried. "How could I fail to see when I carried you from the town?"

Angrily he parted the back of Jonathan's tunic to wash the wounds. Freed of encumbering cloth, amber wings expanded like flames into the air, the great burning glories of the time beyond remembering when the dead ascended, unwearied, to the Celestial Vineyard.

It is a dream, he thought. I sleep and miracles come to taunt me. (But what had Jonathan said? *"Perhaps you will find a sign...."*)

One of the men from Jabesh-Gilead had wakened to David's song and walked, unnoticed, to stand beside him.

He stared in wonderment at the sudden wings.

"The Goddess?" he asked.

"She must have called to him."

"I have heard of such things. There is a place where they go to meet her, those whom she calls. Sirens, and others too who have loved her in life."

"The Celestial Vineyard?"

"It has many names. But it is not like Sheol. It lies above us, does it not? Beyond *them*." He pointed to the stars, which no longer seemed cold and uncompanionable, but friendly torches against the Liliths and the Night Stalkers. North Star, Dog Star, Great Bear ...

I will greet them when Jonathan comes to find me, he

thought. *Yahweh, be with me and the queen I love. Forgive us; accept our forgiveness.*

Now I must find a throne and join the mountains to the sea.

ACKNOWLEDGMENTS

For *How Are the Mighty Fallen*, I am greatly indebted to many sources, novelists more than scholars. To me, the finest Biblical novel ever written is *David the King*, by Gladys Schmitt, who has given me insights and inspiration. I have not presumed to compete with her epic treatment; I have attempted a microcosm, not a macrocosm. She told the entire story of David; I have told only about the few years of his friendship with Jonathan.

Scholars and general readers still dispute the question: Were David and Jonathan lovers as well as friends? The King James and most other English translations obscure the point. Guided by a curious but convincing book called *Greek Love*, I read a translation from the oldest Hebrew Bible, the Masoretic, which treats the relationship between the two young men in language as passionate as any to be found in the Song of Solomon. *How Are the Mighty Fallen*, then, is the story of a love between men. Shocking? Not when you know the men. David was a great poet and a great leader. Jonathan was a deeply gentle man in a harsh, ungentle age. In loving each other, so it seemed to me, they flouted the laws of Israel but obeyed a deity beyond their tribal god Yahweh or, more familiarly if less correctly, Jehovah. I have chosen to call her Ashtoreth, the Goddess, or the Lady.

The rhymed poems in my text belong to me, and I reprint them with the permission of *The Dalhousie Review, Wings, Lyric, The New York Times*, and Achille St. Onge, Publisher. Some of the unrhymed poems are also my own work, while others are quoted from the King James Bible. Readers may be surprised when I attribute part of the Song of Solomon to David. It is generally accepted, however, that Solomon did not write the Song; perhaps he collected several smaller songs, predating him by many years, into a unified whole. One of these songs I have given to David, who, it is possible, may have written all of them, since he is incomparably the finest poet in the Old Testament.